Dedalus Euro Shorts
General Editor: Mike Mitchell

Dedalus Euro Shorts is a new series. Short European fiction which can be read from cover to cover on Euro Star or on a short flight.

Martin Prinz

On the Run

Translated by Mike Mitchell

Dedalus

Dedalus would like to thank the Section with responsibility for the Arts in the Austrian Federal Chancellor's Office and The Arts Council England in Cambridge for their assistance in producing this book.

BUNDESKANZLERAMT ▪ KUNST

Published in the UK by Dedalus Ltd, Langford Lodge,
St Judith's Lane, Sawtry, Cambs, PE28 5XE
email: info@dedalusbooks.com
www.dedalusbooks.com

ISBN 1 903517 36 2

Dedalus is distributed in the United States by SCB Distributors,
15608 South New Century Drive, Gardena, California 90248
email: info@scbdistributors.com   web site: www.scbdistributors.com

Dedalus is distributed in Australia & New Zealand by Peribo Pty Ltd,
58 Beaumont Road, Mount Kuring-gai N.S.W. 2080
email: peribo@bigpond.com

Dedalus is distributed in Canada by Marginal Distribution,
695 Westney Road South, Suite 14 Ajax, Ontario, LI6 6M9
web site: www.marginalbook.com

First published in Austria in 2002
First published by Dedalus in 2005

Der Räuber © Jung und Jung 2002
Translation copyright © Mike Mitchell 2005

The right of Martin Prinz to be identified as the author of this book and of Mike Mitchell to be identified as the translator of this work has been asserted by them in accordance with the Copyright, Designs and Patent Acts, 1988.

Printed in Finland by WS Bookwell
Typeset by RefineCatch Limited, Bungay, Suffolk

A C.I.P. listing for this book is available on request.

THE AUTHOR

Martin Prinz was born in Vienna in 1973. He studied German and Theatre and now teaches at the Institute for Theatre, Film and Media Studies in Vienna.

On the Run is his first novel and was enthusiastically received in Austria and Germany; Wendelin Schmidt-Dengler called it a 'debut that merits the parallels drawn with Kafka's works'. Like the hero of *On the Run*, Martin Prinz is a keen marathon runner.

THE TRANSLATOR

Mike Mitchell is one of Dedalus's editorial directors and is responsible for the Dedalus translation programme. His publications include *The Dedalus Book of Austrian Fantasy*, *Peter Hacks: Drama for a Socialist Society* and *Austria* in the World Bibliographical Series. His translation of Rosendorfer's *Letters Back to Ancient China* won the 1998 Schlegel-Tieck Translation Prize after having been shortlisted in previous years for his translations of *Stephanie* by Herbert Rosendorfer and *The Golem* by Gustav Meyrink. His translation of *Simplicissimus* was shortlisted for The Weidenfeld Translation Prize in 1999 and *The Other Side* by Alfred Kubin in 2000.

He has translated the following books for Dedalus from German: five novels by Gustav Mayrink, three novels by Johann Grimmelshausen, three novels by Herbert Rosendorfer, two novels by Herman Unger, *The Great Bagarozy* by Helmut Krausser, *The Road to Darkness* by Paul Leppin, and *The Other Side* by Alfred Kubin. From French he has translated for Dedalus two novels by Mercedes Deambrosis and *Bruges-la-Morte* by Georges Rodenbach.

Titles available in the Dedalus Euro Shorts series

Lobster – Guillame Lecasble

An Afternoon with Rock Hudson – Mercedes Deambrosis

On the Run – Martin Prinz

l will not let myself tire
Kafka, Diaries

.

THE ROBBER ESCAPES

All at once the air filling his lungs made them light as a balloon. Having been brought to the interview room for his final interrogation on 12 November 1988, Rettenberger, the bank robber, nimbly jumped up onto one of the desks. None of the three police officers moved. One clutched the thermos flask Rettenberger had hurled at him, like a ball he had just managed to catch. The two others seemed to be trapped in their shock and could only watch as Rettenberger, leaping from one table to the next, disappeared through the half-open window.

Rettenberger jumped before he had even given himself time to look down. Perhaps he felt a brief spurt of relief when he saw the roof of the car coming towards him in the darkness. A first intimation of safety: he would not break his legs. The car roof crumpled and buckled, cushioning his fall with a thunderous crash. Rettenberger looked round the yard. He let the air out of his lungs, but even as he breathed in again, panic mounted, the surrounding walls of the police station closed in. One step, then another and he was down from the car roof, making for the exit. Out in the street there was a cold wind against him. He could scarcely breathe.

Rettenberger sped past the front of the police station, along Rennweg, heading out of the city. Every stride as he pushed off from the ground was fuelled by the urge to escape, but his lungs were pressing up into his throat more and more. An icy wind cut through his trousers and thin pullover; his whole body was in the grip of the cold. He was running as fast as he could, yet he could hardly fend off the creeping paralysis. Every second he was expecting the moment when a long column of police cars would come shooting out of the Rennweg station. When that happened he would stop, try to walk along casually and slip as quickly as possible into a door-way or a side street. But he was afraid that when the moment came he would be unable to walk, would just collapse in a heap. Quivering and hardly able to breathe. All his pursuers would have to do would be to pick him up off the pavement.

Then the solid masonry of the prison walls would still be round him, he would just have thrown himself against them one more time, all his hope exhausted in that one unrealisable longing. In prison all desire withered away. In such a restricted space every movement of necessity turns in on your own body. You become calm and apathetic. The walls don't just lock you in, they take your speech, breathing and heartbeat as well, leave you without a life of your own. They are a second skin, a face, a cynical smirk.

There were few people in the street, hardly any cars. It was strangely quiet. While most people were at home, eating dinner or listening to the news on television, those who were out in the streets that Saturday evening did not concern themselves with what was going on around them. Rettenberger's ear kept listening behind him while his hopes dashed on ahead to the crossing: he had to reach it. Running like this, in desperation, he could not get his breath properly, every stride was an effort, but still he pressed on with all the strength he could command. As long as he was still on Rennweg, the column of pursuers only needed to split up, to check the street in either direction, towards the city centre and away from it. They might just manage that. I'm running for my life. Panting, he forced the words out of his mouth, but all that came was a mumble. Yet he felt like shouting out, to break the silence of the street and the passers-by, then immediately running over his own shouts, as if he would have to stifle them. I'm running away. The sentence kept coming, scarcely audible, with every stride he took. And speaking noticeably improved his supply of air, the words passed more easily through the constriction in his throat, the barrier formed by his mute fear, even smoothing over the haste in his breathing.

In the middle of the night of Thursday, 12 August 1985, Rettenberger went to the flat of his fellow student, Erwin Kollhammer, and shot him from close range. It was not until three years later that Rettenberger was linked with the murder. While he was on the run, the newspapers would say that he couldn't stand Kollhammer's perpetual smoking during break on the course in business finance they were both attending. And along with other conjectures about the wanted man, they reported that

Rettenberger kept his hands well manicured and that his voice became shrill when he was excited.

At the Rennweg-Landstrasser Hauptstrasse crossing he could run off to the left, towards the Prater, an area he knew like the back of his hand, or continue down Rennweg to the Central Cemetery. However when, just before the crossing, he heard the first police siren behind him, he turned off to the right without further reflection, ran under the railway bridge and hid in the bushes on the railway embankment beyond. There were police cars everywhere. Instead of the calm glow of evening on the Rennweg that had been so peaceful a moment ago, the flashing lights sent jittery flickers of blue swirling through the dark, like the gleam of a thousand eyes. Rettenberger was shivering, he was literally shaking. Despite that, he became calmer. He breathed in deeply. Slowly he brought himself under control. He'd warm up again eventually. He just had to get moving again. They wouldn't catch him that quickly. And things did quieten down. The blue flashing lights disappeared. He stood up and continued down the street that ran along the railway embankment. Ahead the gatehouse of St Marx Cemetery appeared.

It was half an hour before midnight when there was a knock on Erwin Kollhammer's door. Kollhammer and his wife Christa, 24, woke up. When the knocking was repeated, Christa Kollhammer asked her husband to go and see what it was. Kollhammer went to the door and the next moment took a round of shot full in the face.

Kollhammer had no chance. When, some minutes later, his wife, terrified by the report of the gun, went to see if her husband was all right, he was already dead. He had bled to death by his own front door. There was no trace of whoever had fired the shot. None of the neighbours had seen anything either. A few did hear the report of the gun, but assumed it was a door being slammed.

After Simmering Station Rettenberger left the railway embankment and headed down Grillgasse in the direction of Laa Hill. It was a wide street with no bushes and he ran on the pavement, past the long row of empty parking places belonging to the main railway workshops. His fear of being caught and arrested on the spot had receded. Instead he gradually began to feel the strain of the uphill stretch, forcing him to concentrate on his stride, his posture. He looked every inch an athlete, not just like a bank robber. He stuck with the short, measured stride he had adopted, he hadn't really got into his running yet.

He reached the railway station at the foot of Laa Hill and ran up the footbridge amid a metallic clatter from the steps. Rettenberger halted. Immediately the clatter stopped. He looked across the track. The contours of the line of hills to the west of Vienna could just be made out, like shadows. On that side the city was protected, tranquil, whilst here, on the southern edge, instead of nestling up against the slopes of Laa Hill, it petered out among the many factories and railway lines around it.

13

Rettenberger shot Kollhammer in the face the moment he opened the door. Kollhammer slumped down at once. Even as he staggered back after he had been hit, the blood was already spurting out of him, then gathered in pools beside the lifeless corpse. And although Rettenberger immediately turned and ran down the stairs, that scene stayed in his mind, like a slow-motion sequence from a film. The shot, Koll-hammer, his face torn to shreds, staggering for a moment, then the thick, warm blood bursting out of him, as if it that was what it had always been trying to do.

Once he had crossed the railway line, Rettenberger could tell from the road surface alone that another world began here. The tarmac was uneven, bumpy and worn, with lots of smooth, slippery patches, a real country road.

Rettenberger ran along the middle of the road. After a curve the climb up Laa Hill began. Behind him the bright glow of Vienna appeared once more. The dark emptiness of the industrial district disappeared in the lights. The city put on a glittering show, and as he ran up the slope of Laa Hill Rettenberger was amazed how even the the most depressed areas were swallowed up in the shining sea. He didn't look back any more. He thought he could feel the warmth of the lights at his back, like a loved one. A loved one watching him leave and wishing him all the best.

In front the road snaked its way uphill fairly steeply, with more and more bends, though it was still too short a stretch for proper hairpins. It was already

levelling out and after one more bend he found himself in the Bohemian Funfair. An old merry-go-
round and swingboats for children. The fairground
was not lit, but he could still see the faded colours,
the red and green. The silence around the empty
booths was eerie, as was the appearance of the
colours in the dark. Between closely planted trees
Rettenberger turned off onto a gravel forestry track
which went past the dodgems to Laa Woods.

With every step he heard the echo of his running
feet. A mocking sound, a forlorn sound, in which there
was nothing for it but to hurry on. After the trees
round the Bohemian Funfair a path led along the
fence of the newly reopened nature park. The gravel
came to an end. In the November cold the vehicle
tracks in the clay were rock hard and put bounce into
his step. It was a pleasure to run here. It must be a
bit like running on a tartan track in one of the big
athletics stadiums. He'd never made it that far. He'd
never become a track athlete, had never wanted to;
he'd always been just a runner.

The night was perfectly calm here too. Only the
regular rhythm of his feet hitting the ground made
its own pathway through the dark. Gradually
Rettenberger found his long stride. For the moment
running had banished the cold from his body. It was
still there outside him, all round, he was pushing it
along in front of him, it bounced off his face. But he
felt warm. Already his legs were striding out almost
automatically as he straightened up more and more,
the power coming from the small of his back, his
hips. He felt free, strong. He imagined the fields

beginning to open out to his left. They stretched away to the lights lining the runways of Schwechat airport. He would have liked to come here more often, just for the sake of these fields, but he preferred the meadows of the Prater, not just because they were so extensive, but also because of all the dogs with their owners there were around on Laa Hill at all hours of the day. Nowhere else had he ever been more afraid of dogs than here. Their physical shape and, perhaps even more, the expressionless faces of their owners, reflected the aggression, desperation and poverty that had oppressed him with their mute presence along the railway track below. In contrast, he found the open fields comforting, the calm, the exhilaration of every movement there. Rettenberger was running easily now, just the tips of his toes touching the ground, as if they could keep him in this world. He knew of no image more expressive of concentration than fields of ripe grain waving in the summer breeze. Running came close to that. If he had not become a bank robber, had found a job instead, perhaps as a draughtsman, would he have come here to train more often, instead of always choosing routes through the dense woods of the Prater? Across there, on the other side of the flat top of the hill, the city had its final fling: detached houses, the eight lanes of the busy Laaer-Berg-Strasse and beyond them, to the west, the tower blocks of the Per Albin Hanson estate. At the end of the path Rettenberger crossed the road and turned down a side street.

On the morning of 13 August 1985 Rettenberger

parks the BMW 320 in Hafnerbach. He stole it during
the night in St Pölten to drive to Mautern, where
Erwin Kollhammer lived. The street is empty.
Rettenberger rubs his eyes, he's spent all night driving around. He winds down the window and sticks
his hand out. The air is pleasantly warm. Opposite,
one of the clerks is opening the Raiffeisen Bank.
Rettenberger takes the paper bag – he stopped in the
previous town to make holes for his eyes – and puts it
over his head. A farmer drives past on his tractor.
Rettenberger takes the bag off again. He has not
made up his mind yet and is annoyed he left his new
mask in Vienna. Finally he takes the gun out from
under the passenger seat, picks up the paper bag and
his holdall, and gets out of the car.

Light was streaming out of all the windows of the
Oberlaa Spa and Hydro. The car park in front and the
one-way drive leading to and from the main entrance
were also dazzlingly bright, like football pitches with
the floodlights on. Apart from him, there seemed
to be no one else in the whole place. Rettenberger
tried to slip past in the shadow of the bushes lining
the car park and drive. If there had been a concert in
the Assembly Rooms, everywhere would have been
swarming with cars and people. In that kind of
throng, no one would have noticed him. He would
have pushed his way through the crowd, as if he had
left something in his car, then disappeared in the
darkness at the edge of the car park. The way things
were, however, even if he kept his head down, he
would still have the whole day-bright glare of the

floodlights focused on him. He'd had enough of hiding. Throwing back his shoulders, Rettenberger strolled across the car park as if he had all the time in the world. He walked like a night-watchman, stared at the windows, the huge eyes of the hotel buildings, imagining the guests sitting there in the light of their televisions, entirely shut off from the world, content after a strenuous day devoted to their health. As long as the televisions were switched on no one would notice him out there. Only the following day, when he was part of the news, would they follow his escape with amazement. Not even the porter, who, like every porter, was sitting with his back to the surveillance cameras, feet up, a cup of coffee in his hand, saw him pass.

'Watch out! I think there's going to be a hold-up at the bank in a few minutes.' It was a farmer, Ludwig Gruber, 60, who phoned this warning of a possible hold-up to Maria Steinperl, the cashier at the Raiffeisen Bank in Hafnerbach near St Pölten, on Tuesday morning. 'I thought the warning was a sick joke,' she said. 'But I was soon laughing on the other side of my face when my husband Dietrich, who happened to be in the bank, called out to me to press the alarm button.' By then the robber was already in the bank. Gruber had been right in his observation. The paper bag the unknown man had pulled over his head was to mask his face. Showing great presence of mind, Dietrich Steinperl blocked the door with his foot. Surprised that he was expected, the gangster turned and fled. He jumped into a metallic blue BMW, registra-

tion N 217 200, that had been stolen the day before.
He got away.

When Rettenberger reached the far end of the car
park, he slipped through the hedge and ran along
the road leading away. The hill lay, like a heavy,
night-black giant, behind the brightly lit health
spa. He still had to get through between Oberlaa
and Unterlaa, but the lights in the two small sub-
urbs were swallowed up in the shadows of the narrow streets, so that the street lamps presented no
danger.

After the bridge over the Liesing, the fields spread
out before him, names he only knew from the map of
the city, stretching far to the south and west, interrupted by small towns and villages. In the summer
they were like a straw-yellow sea lapping at the edge
of the city: Obere Scheibe, Untere Scheibe, Lachfeld,
Sandgrubenfeld, Hennersdorfer Heide, Tändelbreite.
Fields, canals, railway lines. The various settlements
tiny points of light among them. It was areas like
this that made you realise country villages were
nothing other than islands.

At last Rettenberger was running freely. He slipped
into the open countryside with long, relaxed strides.
They carried him forward easily, he felt pride at the
way his movements had regained their smoothness.
He was running effortlessly, not breathlessly, and
that gave him tremendous pleasure.

Beyond the bridge – he was out of Unterlaa now –
even the sparse contours of the fields disappeared.
The landscape was swallowed up in the darkness

around him, only re-emerging in motion, in the few metres he could see in front of him.

His face appears as a sole smudge of brightness on the canvas of a night like that. His deep-set eyes are tunnels that bore into the blackness, even carrying part of the dark on into the daylight, while the gleam of the bank robber's face, shy and at the same time slightly disturbed, brings daylight into the night. His face is narrow and boyish, with cheek-bones like shoulders, slim shoulders that present the bank robber's every smile, every glance to the world. The bank robber is fearful of his own fragility, feels his face as a mask, glassy, wafer-thin. He never claps his hand to his forehead, taps his head or drums on his lips with his index and middle finger. He gently lays his face on his half-open hand to rest. And like a flame, he often vanishes in the darkness of the night.

At midday on Friday, 11 November 1988, there was a knock at the door of his flat. He had just had a shower after his morning run in the Prater and was sitting in the living room reading the newspaper. When he heard the knock, he stood up and went to the door, knowing already what was awaiting him. He had a quick look through the peephole. All he could have done would have been to jump out of the window, but he lived much too high up for that.

He opened the door. The police officers came up to him and just said his name, at the same time ordering him to stand against the wall. By then he was already afraid it wasn't just the bank robberies they were investigating, but the murder as well. They led him away. He was calm and composed. His arrest had obviously been prepared several days ago, the investigating officers had probably gathered all the evidence already and had a clear picture of all his robberies, from the first two, only moderately successful ones in Hafnerbach and Gross-Sierning, to the hat-trick of hold-ups in February of that year which had taken him in one single day from Simmering to Kirchstetten to Markersdorf. Three hold-ups in one day! He had simply flown from one to the next, had quite possibly already been in Markersdorf before the local police had got a clear idea of what had happened during the robbery in Kirchstetten. Then, one month later, the crowning achievement of his career: two million schillings from the Krottenbachstrasse branch of the Creditanstalt in Vienna, a million the next day from the Gärtner Bank in Simmering, and another million the day after that from the Creditanstalt in Dornbach. Each one of the three hold-ups had been a model of calm and control. It was a performance he was happy with. By this time, in contrast to the bank robbery just after he'd finished school more than ten years ago, when he had been caught in the act and sent to prison, he had not made any silly mistakes out of nervousness or fear. But once the detectives had established a connection between all these hold-ups – the Ronald Reagan mask he had been using since Gross-Sierning, the shorter and shorter intervals between them – there had been bound to come a point where they stuck to his heels like a shadow which couldn't be shaken off. He wondered whether they did actually connect him with the murder. He walked meekly along in front of the policemen, wishing he could simply disappear from sight. Perhaps the contempt he could see in their looks was directed at the murderer?

Rettenberger couldn't tell how long he had been running through the fields any more. He was amazed he had not lost his way in the network of gravel tracks. At one point the lights of Vösendorf had saved him from going badly wrong. Eventually he had followed another railway line, running southwards for a while in the shadow of the embankment, which gave him a feeling of security. After Laxenburg there were a few meadows to cross before the first vineyards finally began. As he reached the B17, Rettenberger felt the relief flood through him even before he crossed the road and slipped out of sight between the vines, bare of grapes at this season. He couldn't get lost here, yet was unlikely to be detected. He saw the lights of Gumpoldskirchen; at short intervals midnight rang out from the churches all round. Some way in front of him the slope began to climb up to the Anninger. He found encouragement in the rows of vines leading straight towards it, like little railway tracks. He accelerated. He had decided not to run round the Anninger or between the so-called 'Baby Matterhorn' and the Little Anninger to Weissenbach or Sparbach. He would take the direct route to the summit. Just as on a training run. He was not worried about the pace, he had regained his strength and fluidity of movement. The month's rest after the hill marathon in Kainach had done him good. There was a powerful spring in his legs once more. His victory, and the ease with which he had left Hones trailing, the langlauf skier who always looked as if it was such an effort, were his best achievements so far. He put the first third of the climb behind him at an even tempo, then started to step up the pace.

As he runs, the bank robber pushes into the nocturnal landscape he has to hurry through. Stride by loping stride, the ground covered accumulates. It happens automatically, each of his movements flowing quite naturally into the next. His escape is there, hurrying along ahead of him, never quite disappearing, like a fleeting thought or a vacant look. As he runs, he is absorbed into the nocturnal landscape, at the same time appearing as part of it with the smooth lift of his knees, the release of his legs as they swing out behind him. His arms prescribe the rhythm. Bent at an angle, they swing back from his chest, then forward again, brushing his hips, drawing his body back up, even as it touches the ground, creating the necessary tension. Thus he determines his pace, the degree of concentration, increases the centrifugal force of his body.

The bank robber accelerates imperceptibly. The slope gets steeper and he goes a touch faster. He has long since left the vineyards behind, now he is running up the hillside. The steeper it gets, the more the upward path is compressed into curves and bends, so that he is almost overwhelmed by the desire to head straight for the summit. But he is still reluctant to entrust himself to the trees. He needs a path, needs to feel its firmness under his feet, to see it shining in the moonlight so as not to give way to despair in the darkness. And the bank robber runs faster still, he feels as if he is about to fly. Every acceleration of the stride pattern on a slope getting steeper and steeper makes you feel as if you are taking off, floating briefly through the air. Perhaps that is what he is running after. He almost floats over the Anninger, putting in one final spurt before the summit. It could be a moment in which the world pauses in its slow turning, stops while the bank robber continues running alone for a brief instant, before the world starts to turn again, binding him firmly to the ground. The next moment he disappears in the trees.

From the top of the Anninger, Rettenberger ran past the Jubilee Tower and along the bed of a stream down to Gaaden and Siegenfeld. It looked as if he could not get enough running, so greedily was he gobbling up the night. He continued through the wooded Heutal to Preinsfeld, even losing his fear of the woods and gazing in astonishment, when he came to the clearing, at the half dozen houses and three fields of the hamlet, which did not even seem to boast a church, only a brightly lit telephone box at the end of the village. Tempting fate, he went boldly along the one street, past the few houses. Thinking of the children and their parents sleeping peacefully, he smiled. Perhaps he had made his escape and was free, perhaps he could stay that way. Confident now, he ran on until he saw the fields of Alland in front of him.

The simple act of running away had formed a kind of protective skin which, after he had managed to shake off his initial panic, seemed to become more and more impenetrable with every stride. Once he was out of the trees and no longer had to concentrate on his immediate surroundings, he neither heard nor saw anything, he simply ran, moving through the night as if he were alone in the world. Nothing less than a blue flashing light and a siren would jolt him out of his dream, put him once more at the mercy of the world, body and soul.

Usually when he ran he always tried, despite the immense distances he covered, to feel he was heading for home. On those long mornings in the Prater, after he had accompanied his girlfriend to work in the city centre, his training runs were the only possible way of approaching the rest of the day. The Fasangarten, the Ameisbügel, the Heustadelwasser, across the Wasserwiese and up to the Jesuitenwiese, usually with people playing football, then back to the Lower Prater, towards Freudenau Racecourse, never on the Main Avenue, always taking the smaller paths. His whole world consisted of runs like that. And more than the satisfaction at the distances covered, it was probably the tiredness that enabled him to put up with all the rest. Enveloped in weariness, he could return to the everyday world, to the shopping, cooking, waiting for his girlfriend and their cosy evenings together.

He had always come back. Even though he had sometimes thought he must keep on running, just to be able to bear his life. This time he would never go back. He was running away and stride by stride the world was disappearing without trace behind him. Rettenberger had reached the first houses of Alland. There was no one about, just as there had been no one in the outskirts of Gaaden. The darkness was his best protection. He was sure he would see the headlights before drivers could see him. If a car should appear round a corner in front of him, he would immediately drop into the ditch or hide behind a tree. But going from a dark country road into even a small town like Alland was like going from a dark corridor into a brightly lit living-room. Even if everyone seemed to be asleep, you could never be sure there was not danger lurking somewhere.

When, just at the beginning of the town, Rettenberger saw a *Bed and Breakfast: Vacancies* sign by a dark unmetalled track leading to the edge of the woods, he suddenly felt that was where he wanted to be. He rang the bell and, after a while, a half-dressed woman opened the door. He said, 'Good evening, do you happen to have a room?' but when she did not answer straight away, fear gripped him again. He managed a 'No? Right then,' and ran off.

They had spent the whole of the Friday afternoon interrogating him. In pairs, in threes, they went through every detail of the hold-ups, slipping in the occasional casual question about the murder of Kollhammer. Not once did they mention the stolen BMW or any evidence connecting him with the killing. Instead they told him how it had affected the family. As they did so, a brief memory came back to mind of how sober and civilised Kollhammer had looked as, his eyes still full of sleep, he had opened the door. He was far more horrified by this memory than by any of the accusations they made. All the time they were besieging him with evidence about the bank robberies. They didn't give him an inch of room to manoeuvre, all around these forceful voices haranguing him, pressing up against him, literally sticking to him. They told him everything about his life, as if they'd been observing him since childhood.

Rettenberger stumbled as he ran away from the bed and breakfast. Fear had gripped him with a sudden shock, as if he had run full tilt into a solid wall. There was clearly nothing left connecting him with other people. All that there was between him and others was fright. He ran down the track to the main road, past the brightly lit petrol station. He felt dizzy.

Back in his cell after the interrogations, he thought he was going to suffocate. From the moment when the policemen stopped going on at him, he felt more and more constricted. His body was so heavy, he sat on the camp bed hardly able to breathe. He could not even cry. There was no way out. This sense of being shut in with no way out was the only thing you could feel in a prison. He was afraid, so afraid that all he wanted was to get away. Even if he had to spend the whole night banging his head against the wall. As hard as he could.

He lay there, wide awake. In the morning he felt

he had not slept a wink. Every single breath had been an effort he had to make to lift the panic that was pressing down on him. His whole body was aching, as it had when he was a child during the periods when he was growing too fast. He could clearly feel the pressure in his bones; he did not just want to break out of the prison, more than anything he wanted to break out of his own body.

Rettenberger stuck to the main road, heading east, back in the direction of Gaaden. For the first few hundred yards he did not even use the pavement but ran down the middle of the road. As he left the houses of Alland behind, he continued along the dead straight road, past the turn-off to the autobahn, along the broad fields below Preinsfeld down into Heiligenkreuz, the headlights on the autobahn cutting through the night like contours along the hillside above. Rettenberger's footsteps echoed through the town. He hurried past the monastery, where a few lights were still on. There was no movement, all was quiet in the houses. After the end of the town there was a long straight stretch up to the top of the next hill.

Gradually he began to forget his pursuers, whom he had seen suddenly threatening him in the startled face of the woman at the bed and breakfast. In a long, hard sprint he pushed against the tarmac, his feet pounding it with such force he was no longer aware whether he was running uphill, downhill, round a bend or along a straight.

After he had raced through Gaaden he eventually

turned west again, out of the narrowing valley that led to Mödling, and after a couple of kilometres came to Sparbach. He passed an outlying estate and several excavated plots with empty spaces between, then came underneath the autobahn, which cut its way through the fields here, and into the centre of the village. The old houses round the church were asleep, taking the same deep breaths as their occupants. But at the edge of the forest he saw the gleam of a row of weekend chalets, set fairly well apart from each other. Rettenberger headed for them. He climbed over the fence into the garden of the first one he came to and made a quick circuit, but he was sure there was no one there – his certainty coming in part from his exhaustion – and climbed in through one of the windows on the forest side.

A robber is flying through the night. Wrapped in darkness, he feels secure in his loneliness. The world outside passes by in silence, a cold wind no longer touching his hot body. Light-footed, he hurries along.

When Rettenberger woke up the next morning, he felt shattered. The night before, after he had broken into the chalet, in a sudden fit of ravenous hunger he had stuffed himself with anything edible he could find and had stayed awake for a long time. Even now he could still feel the restlessness of his escape run. Perhaps he would never be entirely free of it. He felt totally exhausted, as if his legs, his whole body had remained in furious motion during his few hours' sleep. The strange bed was sodden, he noticed that as he lay there, half awake, slowly getting cold, his body sticking to the sheets. His eyes were so puffy he could feel the pressure of the rings under them on his face.

Rettenberger got up and was immediately aware of his legs. The previous day he had run more than fifty kilometres, in ordinary shoes, with lots of uphill stretches. His leg muscles were taut, stiff, they really hurt and he was proud of himself. Everything had gone right the previous day. He had escaped from the prison and his pursuers. The first steps he took away from his bed were unsteady, but that would pass.

In the kitchen he made himself some tea. During the night before he had sat there in the dark until his body calmed down, his heart stopped beating so wildly and his headache began to wear off. He found some aspirin in a drawer. A headache after great exertions like that was something he was familiar with, but this time it was mainly the mass of doubts immediately crowding into his mind again the moment his non-stop running ceased.

'The desire for freedom is unusually strong in this man. He never comes across as an unpleasant person, but whenever he sees the slightest chance of escaping he becomes completely blind to anything else. And since he is intelligent, he is highly dangerous in that kind of situation.'

The man who provided this description of the murderer and bank robber, Johann Rettenberger, knows him better than almost anyone else. Kurt Reiner is the director of Stein Prison and had Rettenberger, imprisoned for repeated robberies, in his care for almost eight years.

Only shortly after he had arrived there, in 1977, he made a frantic, though unsuccessful attempt to escape while he was being taken to hospital. He was transferred to the security wing, from which he attempted a second break-out in 1981. He failed once more when the ropes and grappling irons he had managed to obtain were discovered.

'The man has nothing to lose, he can expect a life sentence next time. He will stop at nothing, we must be prepared for further hold-ups,' said a police spokesman, warning the public to beware of 'Marathon Man' on the run, the cause of the biggest operation ever in the history of the Austrian police.

Rettenberger drank his peppermint tea in careful sips. It was refreshing. As he drank, he looked out of the window. Light rain was falling. He was surprised it was not snowing, given how cold it had been during the night. But when he had a look at the driveway, he saw that the ground was like a sheet of glass. He was glad to be sitting inside. Outside the church bells were ringing. He put his feet up on another chair and went on looking out of the window. It was a grey morning. He could easily imagine what the village looked like. He came from the country himself, somewhere else he could never go back to. He imagined people flocking to church from all over Sparbach, families, pensioners, the pious old women. The streets would probably be deserted during mass. But that would make them all the more dangerous. The few who had to stay at home because they were ill or too old would keep a watchful eye on the streets for those who were late or heading straight for the inn without bothering with church.

For the moment all he could do was wait. But simply sitting there looking out of the window would be unbearable. Time seemed to have stood still on the stretch of meadow he could see from the window. When the church bells were not ringing, the sirens going off for the regular Saturday fire practice or a car happened to be passing through, time hardly seemed to pass in places like this, locking you in wherever you happened to be. He needed to be doing something. But he was much too exhausted. He was exhausted from the previous night and, if truth were told, from the day to come already. He must not give up now.

A robber wakes up in the morning and faces the day with a determined expression. A robber must use it to frighten the day ahead but must not let anything frighten him. A true robber is always wide awake, only sleeps to pass the time, and is always on the lookout, even when he is asleep.

During the morning Rettenberger went through the house, not looking for anything specific. Slowly his head began to clear. Now he could concentrate again. The house smelt of money and yet looked dilapidated. There were carpets everywhere, overlapping, so many that it looked as if they had needed to cover the floor twice over. Nothing creaked when he walked over them. There were various antlers hanging on the walls of the hallway and stairs, in one corner he found a stuffed marmot. That fitted. As did the master's study, which looked downright ostentatious: a lot of leather, a lot of brown and photos of a small, crafty-looking man in full hunting gear. Presumably he would normally be sitting at this desk at weekends, had only stayed away because of the bad weather, was in Vienna moaning about the cold and rain.

Johann Rettenberger, 30, from St Leonhard am Forst in Lower Austria, last resident in Vienna-Simmering, is considered very intelligent and comes from a very good home. His family, mostly highly respected people with a university degree, are horrified. Not surprisingly, everyone was talking about Johann Rettenberger in the inns around St Leonhard. No one would have believed Rettenberger, who was a quiet boy, only known for his sporting prowess, capable of a series of crimes like that.

Rettenberger went back downstairs. He felt most comfortable in the kitchen. There everything had obviously stayed the same for the last twenty years: white cupboards, red work surfaces, no hunting trophies. All the objects there looked used, but the room was bright and pleasant. He sat down at the table, clasped his hands behind his head and stared into space. He had to eat something, above all he had to drink. Otherwise there was nothing to do but wait for nightfall. He did not know whether the police were on his trail, he had not seen any patrol cars yet. He was sure that even if the woman at the bed and breakfast in Alland had heard of his escape over the radio she had not said anything about his confused attempt to take a room there. He had no idea why, but he was sure.

After they had spent the Friday bombarding him with questions and facts about the hold-ups, but not with any real evidence connecting him to the murder, on Saturday the police concentrated more and more on Kollhammer. Rettenberger tried to gain time by confessing to one of the hold-ups, but denied everything connected with Kollhammer's murder, as well as his first robbery, in Hafnerbach, on the following day. It was probably to his advantage that he had not used the mask for that. The amateur paper bag was some use after all. He had only become Ronald Reagan over two years later in Gross-Sierning. And Ronald Reagan was a different person. His interrogators fell for it. The only factor linking the hold-ups and the murder was the pump-action shotgun. But others used shotguns as well. It was not going to be that easy for them to pin the murder on him. They had obviously arrested his girl friend too and she, as was clear from the start, had told them everything she knew.

Erika was a nice girl. Perhaps he had never really loved her, sometimes even hated her, but in a way she had still been the best thing in his life. She came from the same town as him, had worked in a very good hotel since she had moved to Vienna, and was always content with everything. He could even imagine it would not bother her too much to spend some time in prison. Erika never seemed unhappy. She probably never was.

Erika knew nothing at all about the murder. That gave him the confidence to hint that he was willing to make a full confession to the robberies, in order to get his interrogators to relax, with the result that they actually took off the handcuffs when he asked if he might have a drink.

36-year-old Erika J.'s world fell apart in the spring when she saw in the newspaper the security-camera pictures of the bank robber with the Ronald-Reagan mask, known everywhere simply as 'Pump-gun Ronnie', and recognised his sports bag and anorak. As soon as she got home from work she told him what she had seen in the paper, that she knew now who he was. Immediately Rettenberger faced her with the decision: leave him or say nothing. She decided to stay with him. He promised her he would not hold up any more banks. She believed him, even depositing part of the proceeds of his robberies with various banks. Then she went away on holiday with him and he told her of his plan to use all the money to allow them to carry out their plan, until then beyond their means, of opening a general store in Hochegg, where her doctor kept suggesting she should move permanently because of her asthma.

Rettenberger spent half the afternoon searching the house for a gun. It had suddenly occurred to him that there might be some firearms there. He started in the study, then rummaged through the living room and kitchen, but could not find one anywhere. There were some old rifles hanging on the wall of the living room, but they were just for decoration, well looked after but probably from the last century and no use to him. Finally, in the cellar he found a box with several toy rifles. One had drawing pins all over the stock. It must be the silver gun from Karl May's Wild West stories. He'd read the books when he was a child. Like their horses, Winnetou's and Old Shatterhand's rifles had been able to perform miracles; even when outnumbered and in tricky situations, they had been superior to the enemy in rapidity and fire-power. Old Shatterhand even had a second rifle. It was so powerful, it was called 'Bearkiller'. Rettenberger went back up and sat in the kitchen. Down in the street there was still nothing of the local police or patrol cars to be seen.

'When he was nineteen and was sent to prison for the first time in 1977, many local people talked about a miscarriage of justice,' a baker in St Leonhard told us. Until only two weeks before, the 3,000 inhabitants of the little town in Lower Austria had still been watching Rettenberger on his extended training runs. Apart from his successes in marathons and other long-distance races, the people of St Leonhard knew nothing about his activities. Before his first crime (a bank hold-up in 1977) the vain and sensitive all-round sportsman was a valued member of the local football team. After his release in 1984, he trained with the club again, otherwise Rettenberger avoided clubs and organisations. He didn't smoke or drink. One thing all the people from the town we questioned were in agreement about: a disturbed family background was definitely not the cause of Rettenberger's deviation from the straight and narrow.

He stood up, walked to and fro. His legs had loosened up, but the feeling of being locked in was oppressive. He must not stay here for long. In houses like this you were found more quickly than you would think. If a neighbour noticed even the smallest irregularity – a noise, a movement at the window – when the owner's car was not in the drive, he would call the local police at once. Rettenberger sat down again. He must wait until the evening before he could risk going out. He must get somewhere where they would not be looking for him. Then he could steal a car, get onto the autobahn and be miles away in no time at all.

In November 1987 Rettenberger held up the Raiffeisen Bank in Gross-Sierning, east of Melk. This time he stayed in the car just for a moment, to gather himself. The mask was in his army-surplus anorak, the gun and the sports bag for the money were ready. He must not hesitate, must dash into the bank with the gun, shout, 'Give us the money' and drive off as quickly as possible. Rettenberger knew the town. He had grown up only fifteen kilometres away. He took one more deep breath, observing himself as he slipped effortlessly into the movements of the great bank robber. With that breath he *was* the robber and the others were afraid of him. He picked up the gun and the bag as if they were the most normal tools in the world, put on the Ronald-Reagan mask and went into the bank.

The first thing the customers at the counter noticed was the shotgun. They hardly registered the mask, only the sawn-off shotgun. At once it's quiet and Rettenberger goes to the counter, growls, 'This is a hold-up! Give us the money,' in as indefinable a Viennese accent as possible, indicating his sports bag with the gun. He is in control. The cashier shoves money across to him, Rettenberger sweeps it into the bag, keeping his gun on the people round him. It's all calm.

At last it started to get dark. Rettenberger searched the house for more clothes. He had to get himself kitted out for going on foot. Presumably there would have been reports about him on the radio and television, and anyone seen on the roads or going across the fields in light city clothes would immediately attract attention. He did not switch on the news, even though that would have told him more about his pursuers. He was sure the reports would just describe him as a murderer. He did not want to hear that, not even, when it came down to it, where the police were looking for him. It would be better for him to concentrate on his escape, he would show them what stamina he had. For going on foot he needed warmer clothes, and after only a brief search he was cursing the owner of the house for being so much shorter and fatter than he was. Finally in the cellar he found an old, reddish-brown leather jacket with a thick astrakhan collar and a black woollen cardigan which more or less fitted. He couldn't find any stronger shoes anywhere, but he was happy enough for the moment, at least he could hide his face in the collar, which would surely not strike anyone as strange in this weather.

Rettenberger also pocketed a penknife, the last pieces of bread and some Dextrosol he found in a coat pocket. He eventually decided that putting on a hat, or one of the fur caps, of which there was no shortage there, would be going too far. He climbed out by the window he had used during the night and set off through the woods to try and find a road.

One of the few people he passed in the rain on the main road to Sittendorf must have thought him suspicious. Shortly afterwards a car drove past, so slowly it looked as if the driver was trying to avoid splashing him. But after it had passed him it did not accelerate. Rettenberger knew straight away what was going to happen. Years ago, before running became fashionable, cars had overtaken him like that, the amused or astonished faces of whole families turned towards him as they slowly drove past. The two men in the car, however, had not looked at him at all. They obviously knew whom they were dealing with. Rettenberger kept walking, he must not stop. Perhaps that would disconcert them slightly. Then the car stopped beside him. Two policemen leapt out, but when they asked him his name it was in friendly tones. Rettenberger answered without hesitation, 'Hartmann, Gerhard Hartmann, Herr Inspektor,' and immediately, even as the officer said 'Well, Herr Hartmann, would you mind putting your hands on the roof of the car?' he really was Herr Hartmann and laughed silently to himself, as he put his hands on the car roof, so little fear of them did he feel. One of the policemen frisked him, the other asked, 'Haven't you got your identity card on you, Herr Hartmann?'

'No,' Rettenberger replied in the same friendly tone, 'I've just arrived and wanted to stretch my legs. I left my wallet in the inn where I'm staying the night.' The two policeman looked at each other, unsure what to do, so he went on to say that he would quite understand if they insisted on driving him back there. 'After all, I've heard about the escaped criminal.'

As if on command, the two policemen, in apparent agreement with his suggestion, turned away. Rettenberger, still with his hands on the car roof, whipped round, knocked the gun out of the hand of one of the policemen, snatched it up and ran off across the fields.

A large-scale operation during the night producing no result, at six o'clock on Monday morning the police set in motion what was must have been the largest manhunt in years. The wooded area around Sparbach was surrounded by almost three hundred police officers, including thirty-five dog handlers and two helicopter crews.

Soon after Rettenberger's second escape, the sound of a gunshot was heard in the forest. However, he had not committed suicide, but was clearly just testing the gun he had taken from the officer. Along with the FN pistol, the criminal acquired thirteen rounds of ammunition.

Following this, the police hourly expected to hear of a car being stolen, a bank robbed or a hostage taken by Rettenberger as the net closed in on him. Already questions were being asked in parliament about the suspect's escape from a police station and about the security of the building. Despite the neat piece of police work that had led to Rettenberger being stopped near Sparbach, the officers who had let Rettenberger get away were threatened with disciplinary proceedings, since one had clearly stood in the other's line of fire.

THE ROBBER IN A TRAP

Rettenberger ran. He was heavy-legged, but he ran as fast as he could. After a few hundred yards in the darkness he went back through the autobahn underpass to the other side of Sparbach. His feet hammered the ground. He ran past the houses and into the woods, and with every stride he felt he was sinking deeper and deeper into the dead leaves and earth between the first trees. He kept the policeman's gun in his hand, holding it close to his body, holding onto it, just as he had grasped it. Perhaps he would never have stopped if he had not suddenly become aware of the pistol. Perhaps he would have kept running until he was completely exhausted, until his heart was no longer pounding, but racing with a very light, fast beat, eventually speeding away from him in one last moment of sharp pain.

Even at the very first stride he had given up all hope of shaking off the pursuit. His body felt sluggish. As he ran, it took almost more effort to keep upright, to restrain the urge to let himself fall down flat, than to move forward. He staggered from one step to the next and eventually stopped, supporting himself against a tree, breathing heavily. There was no point in running away. At least he was in the woods here, what more did he want?

All the time he was holding the gun, which he had

caught in one last moment of lightness. Before his eyes had adjusted to the darkness in the woods he could not see it, only feel it with his hand. Holding it in his right hand, he aimed at the trees all around, then ducked behind a tree and sprang out, holding both arms outstretched, he stood there, in the middle of Sparbach Woods, legs apart like American cops. Rettenberger felt the magazine, emptied it, refilled it. He had thirteen bullets. With the first – the idea suddenly came to him – he would draw attention to himself. He was far from being caught yet. He aimed down at the ground a little way in front of him and pulled the trigger. The shot echoed through the forest, would certainly be heard clearly outside as well. He had twelve left. The hunt was up. They would have their work cut out finding him here.

Satisfied with himself, he set off up the hill. The trees in front stood out in the blackness. It was still night-dark in the woods, but the trees gradually developed distinct colours, a somewhat richer black. He was glad the wood was on a slope, it made it easier to follow a straight line if he kept climbing. On the flat he would have ended up going round in a circle. He found walking easier than the running had been. It hardly tired him at all. Above all, he did not feel as helpless as when he was simply running away. For the second time he knew his pursuers were close. While yesterday, having just given the police the slip in the city, he had grown in confidence during his night-time flight, running here had lost all its dignity. This running away turned him into a tiny, insignificant figure.

Rettenberger stepped carefully, being prepared for a possible slip each time he put his foot down. Only after he had found a firm foothold did he transfer his weight, at the same time keeping his knee bent and relaxed to counter any slipping that might still occur. He was walking with almost the same even gait as climbers at high altitudes. The gun in his right hand, he went up the slope step by step, breathing calmly and slowly casting off the fear of being hopelessly trapped, which had so gripped him while he had been running. Walking too had a rhythm of its own and he felt a touch easier; in walking the chest was not proudly borne in front, as in running, it went with the rest of the body, determining the rhythm with its rise and fall.

Then he heard his pursuers in the forest, like a hurricane rising. Boughs snapped with a crack, he heard shouts and orders from far off. All the feet hitting the ground, all the bodies brushing through the branches sounded like the beginning of a storm. At first Rettenberger just continued walking. Down below there was a whole pack of policemen running around, he was sure that now it was only the local police, they would not want help from the Vienna force. He kept walking, it was not a hare-and-hounds race any more. On the other side of the hill there were presumably just as many policemen in close formation, marching up through the trees in their heavy boots. If he started running away here, he would be there all the more quickly. It was eerie, suddenly to find himself in the woods with so many people. Even his own steps made a loud rustling noise in the thick layer of dead leaves. The hill ought to tremble under the onslaught. But a hill does not tremble.

Once, when Rettenberger turned round, he saw the torches, their clearly defined beams cutting through the tree trunks. They did not reach as far as him. There were still too many trees between them. He imagined how often it must appear to the police that they had caught sight of him behind a tree, only to realise the next moment that what they thought was the bank robber was just a misshapen tree-trunk. In the light from the torches everything was reduced to the play of light and shade. He could stay hidden in that for a while longer. No one came close to him. Already the police officers, perhaps distracted by too many of these phantasms, seemed to be less persistent in their pursuit, were no longer pouring up the hillside like an all-engulfing tidal wave. They were looking for him literally step by step, hardly making any forward progress at all. Perhaps it was not necessary for them to find him straight away, since they had him so securely encircled. Again that gave him more time. He sat down, watching and listening to the search for him for a while.

A robber is sitting, surrounded, on a hill. For the moment the place he is sitting, the dark forest, is still an island. The night is cold, the sky clear and starry. The roads all round slowly fill up with police vans and minibuses. It is a kind of warfare. In the moonlight a landscape of greys and silvers and bright blacks gradually opens out. The robber smiles as he sits in the darkness watching his pursuers. A robber always fights with the moon on his side. He sits there and smiles. That is warfare too. Now it is the others' turn to make a move.

Soon it was all over. The lights disappeared, the woods fell silent. Rettenberger imagined them gathering in the fields below, the senior officers talking, making a grand plan, while the search parties were being served food or sitting in the darkness, just like him, at road blocks round the hill. Once he had calmed down after the excitement of the chase, he realised how exhausted he was. He had a long night out in the open ahead of him, and it could even get a few degrees colder. Presumably they were simply waiting for the solitude and the icy cold to get to him, to induce him to make a rash attempt to break through the cordon. He was determined not to make it easy for them. He would stick it out here. He was safe in the woods, at least during the hours of darkness. But he must on no account stay sitting here. For one thing, it was too cold. But he had calmed down, that was something. He stood up, turned to face the slope, like someone taking one last deep breath before a long dive, and strode on, in the same rhythm as before. Walking had taken over his whole body.

After a while Rettenberger reached the hilltop. He looked down on the lights of Gaaden. From a distance the place appeared quiet, he could not tell whether there were search parties there, in tents or a hall. He turned right along the ridge path, heading in what he assumed was a westerly direction. Soon he came to a wayside pillar with an image of Mary. He always found these light-blue-or-pink-painted shrines for the adoration of the Virgin nauseating. Going along the ridge, he reached the highest point of the low, elongated hill, the Eichkogel, as he learnt after straining his eyes at a sign, 407 metres above sea level. He went on a little way, until he was sure the path only continued downhill. Eventually he was looking down on the next village, Sittendorf, where he had been heading earlier in the evening. And there, not far from the autobahn, he did indeed see that the police had set up camp. He turned back.

After the wayside shrine, he came to another crossing; the path to the left presumably went back to Sparbach, while one to the right headed down towards Gaaden. Rettenberger carried straight on. There was a downhill stretch, then the ridge path was level for a while until, after a short climb, he came to the Schwarzkopf, 396 metres above sea level. Here the woods fell away steeply to a narrow valley leading back to Sparbach. He could see the turn-off from the main road to Gaaden. Beyond the bridge was a police van, with two of the men standing by it, talking. The silence of the valley carried their words up to him with positively unreal clarity.

On 19 February 1988, Rettenberger, carrying his large sports bag, was strolling through the area of Schwechat, to the south-east of Vienna, where the official buildings were situated. He had set off shortly after seven. He made a circuit of the Regional

Council Offices, the Town Hall, the District Courts. He was surprised at the exaggeratedly relaxed and cheerful expressions on the faces of the officials. It seemed to him they were consciously trying to encourage each other before disappearing into their offices. You had to feel sorry for them.

It looked as if it was going to be a fine, sunny day. It was cold, windless. There was a thick, grey-brown crust of ice on the pavements; the streets were free of snow, but still covered with a thin, whitish layer of ice-crystals from the night. The sun was slowly rising, shining between the buildings. It was as if the grey morning had been blown away. Rettenberger had to screw his eyes up. He tried to see out of the corner of his eye whether there were keys in the cars that had been parked by shoppers. He knew he had to be patient, to wait for a lucky chance. Then he had to focus immediately and act quickly. To the east was the extensive site of the refinery, shining in the sun, that was perceptibly higher now. At last, as he was heading towards the town hall square, he saw a car that was double parked. He resisted the urge to go straight towards it; instead he strolled past on the pavement in such a way that he could see whether the key was actually in the ignition. After he had ascertained that it was, he stepped out into the street, approaching the car from behind, as if he was going to cross diagonally, then, when he reached the door, slipped into the driving seat.

From the Schwarzkopf, Rettenberger went back towards the Eichkogel. He recognised some places on the path. It meandered along in the moonlight, like a thread of mist in the silver-grey light, with the woods falling away to either side, blocks of darkness, dense and black. He carried the words the policemen below had spoken along with him in his head, like music. He heard them as a series of notes, as a tune as he went along, as music to walk by while they talked, perhaps about him, the bank robber.

He passed the wayside shrine for the third time, he was already familiar with the side paths. He glanced briefly at the Virgin. Despite his feelings he said, 'Holy Mary,' as he walked past, as a joke, his words already forcing their way in among the talk about the bank robber, 'Holy Mary, Mother of God, pray for us sinners.' That, or something like it, was what his mother used to pray, what the old women in church used to mumble, that was how they imagined living and dying in their singsong that still echoed in his ears. It was far too easy to see something in this perpetual refrain, it was so easy it was almost painful. It's always the easy things that hurt, he thought. Death, life, perhaps longing too. Or perhaps not longing any more, by now that was too far removed from the easy things. He must not say 'Mother of God' now, otherwise the wheel would start turning again, and all he could do would be to laugh, to laugh or to cry out, to cry out loud into the trees and to shoot the gun. But then the wild chase would start all over again, and that would be much too soon.

The engine was running, he had thrown his bag onto the passenger seat. There were two or three cars coming from the right, then there was a gap, he had to pull out into it to get into the stream of traffic and already he was almost too far away to be seen as he drove out of Schwechat towards Vienna. Now everything was going like clockwork. Assuming the owner hadn't managed to catch a glimpse of him at the last moment, he could have driven off in one of several directions and there was no immediate danger of pursuit. By the time the theft had been reported to the local police station, he would have ditched the car. But the next moment everything threatened to go wrong. The barriers were down at the level crossing, there was no train in sight and a long queue of cars already waiting. It startled Rettenberger out of the complacency he had sunk into as he happily drove along, and he began feverishly to look for an alternative. But turning left before the barrier into Kledringer Strasse and making a big detour, along Laaer-Berg-Strasse and past the Southern Railway Station to Simmering, would play havoc with his plan to drive straight from Schwechat to the Creditanstalt Bank in Simmering. He stayed in the queue at the level crossing, unable to decide what to do, but then after only a short time the barrier went up without a train having passed, and the cars started to move. Rettenberger drove off too, still in the grip of the shock, though no one noticed that, he looked like all the others in their cars who were now driving past the Central Cemetery in the direction of the city centre.

A robber walks along a hill. He goes from the Schwarzkopf to the Eichkogel. From the Eichkogel to the Schwarzkopf. He ignores the side paths, keeps wandering back and forth. In one particular he resembles hikers; when they walk it is not merely a method of getting somewhere, it is a necessity for them. A hiker belongs to his hill, he does not just know it, he can literally sense it. He recognises the unevennesses on the path even before his soles touch the ground, so that he flies over it. A hiker walks along a hill because without the hill light-footedness is impossible. And he whistles his song like a robber, drifting along happily in the wake of the notes, since that is the only way he can get into a new tune.

Then Rettenberger started counting the house numbers. He was at number 109, the Creditanstalt was 45. He braced his hands against the steering wheel, glanced quickly at the passenger seat. Everything was there, including his gun. If he made a big haul this time, the mask would finally appear in the newspapers. He was Ronald Reagan, the bank robber. At number 73 he began to look out for the CA sign. In the city there was usually a parking space in front of the banks reserved for vehicles delivering and collecting money. Which in a way is what he would be doing. At number 65 he could still see nothing, nor at 59. At 53 he thought the loading bay already had cars parked in it, but it was just that his view was obstructed. He signalled, slipped into the long parking space outside the bank, left the car with the radiator pointing towards the street, ready for his getaway, switched off the engine and, since he was sure there wouldn't be another car-thief here, left the key in the ignition, just as the man he had stolen it from had. He leapt out of the car, knelt down on the pavement like a 100-metre runner, took the mask out of his bag, put it on, grasped his shotgun and ran into the bank with the bag in his other hand.

A robber creeps through the woods on tiptoe. He does not just stick to the paths, in that he is different from a hiker. Perhaps. A robber creeps all over the place. He hears every rustle, every crack. He never stops, he is always listening to the darkness. Birds flutter in the branches, mice scurry through the dead leaves. Can he hear foxes and badgers too? The tree-trunks are a shimmer of black and grey in the moonlight. The robber flits from tree to tree, he darts uphill, downhill, jumps between the trees, whistling as he goes, leaving the paths behind, following his song.

At 8.19 Rettenberger is in the bank with his gun. Immediately he has the three clerks covered, as well as the handful of customers. It is very quiet. He takes a few steps towards the cash desk, also directing the three employees there as he says, not too loudly, but clearly, 'It's a hold-up.' Straight away the woman at the cash desk takes all the money out of the drawer under the counter, but this time that is not enough for him and he is astonished at how decisive he sounds when he says, in his assumed Viennese accent, 'Not from there – behind you, the safe!' She turns round. 'Hurry up or I'll shoot,' he adds, but by then she's opened the safe and starts stuffing the money into his sports bag.

Once more the gun is sufficient to keep everyone under control and dictate the speed at which the cashier goes about her task. He is master of the situation. Cautiously she pushes the bag across to him. He drops down onto one knee, almost like a dancer, picks up the now heavy bag in his left hand without taking his eye off the people, walks backwards to the door, not needing to say anything, so menacing is the silence that has developed, turns round, runs out through the glass doors, which part automatically, like a stage curtain, to the car and, pulling the mask off his face, drives away.

It was still dark. Rettenberger no longer had any idea what time it might be, no more than he knew how many times he had gone from the Schwarzkopf to the Eichkogel and back. He had long since lost all physical awareness of putting one foot in front of the other. While at the beginning he had been like a swimmer, unceasingly drawn up and down the pool, in constant motion, letting himself be carried along had turned it into a wide sea, full of imaginings, fancies and a sleep-walker's dreams. Nothing was moving anywhere on the hill. Rettenberger stood still for a moment. Dawn had begun to break, imperceptibly, the moon had gone pale, transparent in the grey sky. The warm silver light had gone from the woods. New, fresh policemen would definitely soon be watching out at the edge of the woods, concentrating on their task, waiting for the order to advance. Rettenberger was trembling. Fortunately he remembered the Dextrosol he still had and ate it. He would have gone along with any policeman, allowed himself to be arrested unresisting. But no one came. Presumably he was sick with tiredness and hunger. This night had taken all the strength he had left out of him. When the sun finally came up he would be able to sit down, but while it was still dark he had to keep moving.

After Rettenberger had parked the car near Laa Hill, he walked home. There he put the bag down in a corner, carefully stashed the money away, poured himself a jug of juice and sat down in the living-room. He was surprised how steady his hands were, even though he felt like jumping for joy. For the first time he really had a lot of money. He was not even going to count it. He sat there for a while, triumphant but not knowing what to do with himself, he was more curious to know what the newspapers would have to say about his mask. Ronald Reagan. He wasn't making things easy for them with that hero of the Western world. But he couldn't have appeared before the security cameras as Andrei Gromyko. What he most wanted to do was to read tomorrow's reports now. He knew that in some strange way it would calm him down as he devoured the text greedily, gathering himself together in the descriptions, letter by letter, word by word, as if it were someone else. He could hardly stand it, sitting there, doing nothing. He couldn't even go running. He couldn't keep dashing all over the place simply to stop the world from falling in on him the moment he stood still. At least now and then he wanted to be able to sit back and calmly observe it in its anxious, frantic labours. There had been moments when that had been possible, when he had read, eager yet detached, about his own exploits in the press. In this context even the murder of Kollhammer had acquired a completely new justification.

He needed some distraction, and that straight away. Otherwise he would be sucked into the void that was threatening to engulf him. Already he could feel a nervous twitching in his fingers. As long as he stayed sitting there, he was afraid of any movement he might make. It was his old fear that at any moment he might implode with a dull thud, vanish without trace, as if he had never been. Running was powerless against it. Perhaps being a bank robber was the only way he could rise above the mundanity of everyday life.

Rettenberger made himself some sandwiches, took a bite, without any great enthusiasm, and sat down in the living-room again. He wouldn't be able to say a single word to his girlfriend when she came home in the evening, wouldn't be able to utter a single sound. He was afraid of Erika, afraid that her closeness, her insistent concern would take away what free space he had, would slowly suffocate him. It was the thought that he would not be able to stand this pressure without killing her that frightened him most of all.

After a short time lying on the bed, hoping to escape the pull of his own restlessness, he finally picked up his empty sports bag, gun and car key, took the lift down to the garage and got into his car.

The moment he started the engine he was a different man and drove off calmly, heading for the South-East Expressway. There was not too much traffic anywhere. At Vösendorf he turned onto the Autobahn Ring Road and drove, steadily but unhurriedly, like a train, to St Pölten. His fear had vanished. As he drove along quickly, the countryside brushed past him with a constant, reassuring touch.

A robber is walking through the night. He steps into the darkness, goes through it as if in a dream and emerges, quiet and unseen, on the other side. There is hoar-frost clinging to the clumps of grass, covering the stones and the brown line of earth that is his path. In the hoar frost everything is frozen until the moment when the sun rises. The first movement of the new day begins in the hoar frost, a tiny drop of water rolling off a leaf in the sunshine.

At first there was a helicopter circling round. He saw another briefly over the Anninger. A third one he heard, but couldn't see. The helicopters were directing the pack in the woods. Now the second onslaught was starting. Once more the hill was trembling, at least for him. Rettenberger was sitting on a bench at a viewpoint between the wayside shrine and the Eichkogel. He had started at the noise of the helicopters, presumably he had finally fallen asleep after all. Once more the sound of the footsteps, the hundredfold panting of men on the move, came up to him like a tidal wave. He could hear a lot more dogs now. And the baying of the hounds fitted in well with his vision of a search party made up of young, hungry police officers.

The helicopter appeared over the hill once again, coming nearer this time. Rettenberger fled back into the trees. Now he was the hare. The sound of traffic from the autobahn below seemed to mock him. He mustn't run wildly hither and thither, but he had to keep moving so he wouldn't suddenly get paralysed with fear. If only he could fly sometimes, his feet skimming over the ground, soundlessly, as if he hardly existed. He hurried on, appearing to plunge right through the noises rushing on ahead of the wave of pursuers that flooded up the slope, using the barking, the cries and orders as cover for his own steps.

He was just about to slip out from behind a tree, when a policeman ran past, two or three metres from him, and kept on running up the slope, without looking to the left or the right. Rettenberger moved a quarter turn back round the tree, sticking to the trunk as if he were part of it and, when after some seconds no others arrived, watched the policeman disappear. From his stride he immediately recognised him as a runner. He was showing the others what it was to run up a hill. It obviously hadn't occurred to him to look around at the same time. He was no danger. That came from below.

Rettenberger pushed off from the tree he had been hiding behind. Presumably the policeman would have reached the path on the ridge and would hear nothing for a while but his own panting, his ears completely enveloped in the exertion of his furious breathing. But the search parties would surely soon be appearing from the steeper part of the slope. He didn't have much time. In desperation he rushed through the trees, as if by running he could hold back the tightening ring of pursuers, even make it vanish. Finally he found himself back on the path along the ridge. And he could not repress a smile when he saw that he had come out right beside the wayside shrine, though the smile was probably just a weird twist of the lips. At any moment the police might appear out of the trees. No more skipping round or slipping past them. Instead of running away, all he wanted to do was to disappear, lie down on the spot and put his hands over his head so that he didn't have to see or hear anything any more.

In the afternoon Rettenberger, his sports bag over his shoulder, strolled round St Pölten. As a schoolboy he'd always been impressed by Kremser Gasse, likewise by the side-streets leading off it to the town hall square or the cathedral square with all their cafes and shops. Actually, though, the town centre was tiny. It seemed to him like a toy model of a city pedestrian precinct. Since he had come out of prison, everything that during his schooldays had been of normal size, or even really large, now seemed strangely small. Presumably the images in his memory were still missing those years when he had been locked away. He found the sight of the town almost moving. The squashed row of two-storey buildings, whose facades and ornamental plasterwork were designed for buildings twice as high. At *Sport Gebath* he looked at the window display; as well as tennis, football and ski equipment, they had proper running shoes, had had them for a long time now. When he had tried to buy some while he was still at school, they had shrugged their shoulders and offered him gym shoes or tennis shoes.

Rettenberger crossed the square outside the cathedral, past another sports shop, *Zentra Sport*, where they had been only slightly better informed, but at least had advised him to try ordering direct from the USA, then he continued along the road towards Wagram on the other side of the river. The February sun was clear and mild, already giving off warmth without being too hot and opening up a bright blue, cloudless sky. It had turned out to be the beautiful day the morning in Schwechat had promised. Rettenberger had a strange feeling of expansiveness inside him, as if he were floating through the world into an empty space that was, just for the moment, free of pressure. No one could touch him. Perhaps at such times you really did have the power to free yourself from everything that oppressed you. The sunny afternoon stretched out in front of him like an invitation. By car it was only a short drive from Wagram to the St Pölten East autobahn slip road. Rettenberger crossed the bridge over the river, his sports bag slung casually over his shoulder, his eye scrutinising the parked cars.

Rettenberger was sitting down, his back against the shrine, with the gun in his lap. He watched his breath coming streaming out of his mouth into the cold morning air as his breathing gradually slowed down after his panic-stricken running. He was already practising indifference, staring into space, exhausted. He was determined not to look at the policemen who would appear any minute now. He did not want to see any relieved or aggressively triumphant faces. He must not give them the satisfaction of mocking him before they took him prisoner. While this was going through his mind, sitting there with his head bowed he had probably already been staring at the crater filled with dead leaves right by his feet for some time without registering it. If that hole – a trench left over from the war, a pit made by a fallen tree – was deep enough to take him, then he might still avoid capture. To Rettenberger it suddenly seemed, miraculously, that fate was on his side. He scrambled over and dipped his hands in, as if it were a pool. It had to be deep enough. And it felt as if it was. An inconspicuous depression. He tried to wriggle his way into it as well as he could. Taking care not to disturb the partly frozen surface, he got under the dead leaves, as if he were slipping under the bedcovers.

Rettenberger used his hand to smooth down the place where he had crept in, though it still wouldn't help him if the dogs came. He had enough air to breathe. He tried to relax; he would have to try to breathe more calmly, otherwise he'd be discovered right away. The hiding place was only good as long as no one looked more closely. But who would imagine he was here, of all places, in the bright morning sun-shine, right next to the path along the ridge? Even dogs wouldn't find him straight away, given the tracks he'd left all over the woods during the night. Perhaps by walking he had managed to cover his own tracks. He at least had always ignored the area behind the shrine each time he went past.

He found the car he needed right at the beginning of Wagram. Apparently parked in a hurry, it stood outside an old people's home. As he walked past he could feel the heat the bonnet was still giving off. He hesitated for a moment. Someone visiting a person in an old folks' home surely had the couple of minutes needed to park properly. Finally he got in and drove off. No one shouted or waved their arms. The road in front was empty too. And as if it had been built precisely for his driving, on the curve up to the autobahn he immediately settled into the right speed for the car to hold the road nicely.

The autobahn to Vienna cut through the landscape before him with the decisive carefulness of a surgeon's knife, opening up vistas on the surrounding countryside, in which even the silence that weighed so heavily on its hills could be heard as an unremitting scream. All that came to him from the scattered villages clustering round their spires and fire stations was the constant yes-yes and all the other hackneyed phrases, the manifestly self-evident clichés with which people in these areas accepted life. He wondered whether they did not sometimes realise the absurdity of such voluntary restriction, asking himself how they could constantly hold back the hatred he would feel in their place, as well as any

other necessary emotion, in the characteristic dull-
ness of the expressions on their faces.

As if all that were an air-cushion he was driving
on, Rettenberger glided inexorably onwards, along
the autobahn that ran straight as an arrow over
the occasional rises between St Pölten and Böheimkirchen. It was only when it reached St Christophen
that the landscape would change, with the increas-
ingly numerous hills heralding the Vienna Woods,
that the carriageway would begin to curve, to weave
more and more distinctly one way then the other as it
ascended the uphill gradients in a fluctuating rhythm
which continued until Vienna, where it went down in
a single long descent to the flat land.

Rettenberger kept to a steady speed, moving in the
rhythm determined by the landscape, like a folk song
over its beat. The setting sun was still shining
brightly in through the rear window. With gentle
pressure on the accelerator, he maintained his speed
over each hill as he sailed along.

The footsteps had already come quite close. He
started to panic at the thought that one of the young
policemen might happen to stumble and simply step
on his head with his heavy boots. Rettenberger tried
to take calm, regular breaths to allay the waves of
fear rising within him. But he could only be really
calm when he was in motion, as when he was running, even during a race, but not when he was lying
down, when he immediately felt locked up inside
himself.

He could hear footsteps everywhere. The closer

they came, the more the unison tramp, which had made the ground literally tremble, separated out into thousands of single footsteps, losing its terror, at least for a short while, as it came to resemble individuals trotting along, rather than the heavy tread of a large body of men. Perhaps the reason the stamp of many boots, approaching like a roll of thunder, had dispersed was that they just could not find him. Any minute now the units from the other side of the hill must be arriving. When they reached the path along the ridge, they would just look at each other and then presumably turn back, empty-handed. At least, that was what he hoped.

Now he could hear the voices of the policemen, their laboured breathing, directly above him. Their talk went back and forth, uninterrupted, like a strong wind. Some were probably leaning against the shrine, others would be standing around on the path. In a sudden fit of exuberance he imagined himself with them, imagined himself walking among them, looking them in the face, looking them up and down, without them noticing, while they waited impatiently for the line of men from Gaaden to appear.

Rettenberger lay very still. He had no difficulty imagining himself as an invisible figure in the middle of his enemies; in the last few years he had become so inconspicuous that he was more accustomed to being ignored than being noticed. It was only rarely that he allowed himself to emerge from this insignificance. His arms aloft as he broke the tape when winning a marathon, registering the applause of the spectators as a distant roar, or during a hold-up, his gun at the ready, accepting the much more fervent attention on the faces of the people there.

He was making such an effort to stay calm that he heard less of the clipped phrases they threw out at each other than he had listening to the two police-men standing at the crossroads below during the night. He found it difficult to keep to unobtrusively shallow breaths. He felt as if the policemen, simply by standing there, were compressing the earth around him, creating huge, solid waves of soil which were slowly and silently burying him. Rettenberger knew that very soon he would have to let out a scream, a scream that would go on until he had no breath left. But the policemen went on standing there, fed up perhaps, but as if they had all the time in the world.

At Böheimkirchen Rettenberger turned off the autobahn, floating like an angel down from the exit to the narrow main road. He drove past two petrol stations and the Raiffeisen grain elevator, but turned right onto a country road before he reached the town centre, and made his way, sticking precisely to the speed limit, through a couple of villages to Kirch-stetten. An enormous number of cars came hurtling towards him, he was even overtaken at risky places. They all wanted to get home. As quickly as possible, like bullets from a gun. He felt sorry for them, and yet he was astonished at the assurance with which all these people moved through life. Rettenberger drove carefully, so as not to draw premature attention to himself, along the main street of Kirchstetten. He would have most liked to burst into song out of pure joy at the carefree atmosphere all around and his own abrupt appearance in it.

At 4.35 pm Rettenberger arrived at the main square, indicated, parked the car at a slight angle outside the Volksbank and picked up his sports bag. Going down on one knee on the pavement, he put the mask on, took out his gun and went into the bank.

'Hold-up!' Customers and bank clerks stare, dumbfounded. Yokels the lot of them, their faces, especially their noses, bright red from the schnapps and cider. As the cashier clumsily stuffs the money into his bag, the thought occurs to him that with colouring like that these peasants wouldn't need masks to hold up a bank; afterwards it'd be impossible to identify them anyway from among the hundreds of other red-complexioned peasants in the area. Rettenberger laughs, and the cashier silently filling his bag starts in shock at this sudden laugh from behind the mask. Finally she pushes the well-filled bag across the counter to him and Rettenberger runs out of the bank and back to the car.

At last the police had gone. What remained, hanging as a threat in the air, was the concentrated downthrust of their presence where they had stood. Rettenberger remained hidden in the leaves, even though he was convinced they had definitely withdrawn. Initially that had seemed the simplest thing to do. But just as he had crept into the dead leaves, now the dead leaves were creeping into him, attaching themselves in their sticky moistness to his body, pulling on him as if they would never leave him. At least as long as he lay there he didn't have to think about what to do next. Perhaps if he didn't move away, nothing would ever happen to him. He could not keep himself convinced of that for long. With a jerk which took an effort he no longer thought he was capable of, he stuck his head out of the leaves and looked round.

The path along the ridge, the shrine, it all looked pristine, as if no one had ever been there. Only the sun dazzled him, shining straight into his eyes, that had adjusted to the shade, so that the path, the grass and the shrine looked very unreal, enveloped in a bright yellow, almost whitish haze. It was very quiet. He felt like jumping up right away with a loud cry, a cry like the whoop of a liberated Indian, at the same time shooting at the leaves as they flew off in all directions. But he had to wriggle carefully out of his lair, taking care not to leave any traces that might later reveal his hiding-place. He didn't know whether he might need it again.

Rettenberger drove out of Kirchstetten, taking the road east through Ollersbach, which soon brought him to the next slip road onto the autobahn. There he changed direction and headed back westwards, towards Salzburg. Again he accelerated up the slip road, feeling the same smooth pull that had sent him positively soaring up onto the autobahn in St Pölten. This time he put his foot down harder, pulled out into the outside lane and hurtled along over the three hills, chasing after the sun, a ball of red gradually sinking into the grey murk of a February evening.

This up-and-down gave him such a sense of security, he would most of all have liked to continue on, past the southern exit to St Pölten and over the hill, beyond which the area he came from would suddenly appear.

Shortly before the St Pölten South exit Rettenberger braked and turned off into the gentle curve of the slip road, but instead of turning left into the town, he took the right fork to Ober-Grafendorf, and turned right again there for Markersdorf. He drove along the country lane, between fields grey with the early evening twilight, getting annoyed that he hardly felt anything, didn't even have a tune running through his head as he so often did when he was running. He reached the town shortly after five.

Rettenberger parks outside the bank in Markersdorf. As he puts on the mask he realises he still has the money from the hold-up in Kirchstetten in his bag. It's too late to empty it, so he grabs it and dashes into the bank with the gun, wondering what the expression on the cashier's face will be when he notices there's already a layer of banknotes in the bag. But the cashier, blind with apprehension and fear, just places the notes, in the usual neat bundles, on top of the others and pushes the heavy bag across the counter. Rettenberger grabs it and dashes off. Outside he feels like jumping for joy.

After he had driven under the autobahn, Rettenberger tried to damp down his sudden euphoria. He stuffed the gun into the bag and zipped it up, making heavy weather of it since he could only use one hand. As he drove past one of the bus stops in

Ober-Grafendorf that he had seen every day on the way to school, he made a sudden decision and turned off into a side street, where he parked the stolen car. Slinging the bag over his shoulder, he strolled back to the bus stop on the main road, for all the world like someone going home from football or gymnastics training.

Rettenberger sat down on the bench. He'd have a wait of no more than twenty minutes for the next bus. He felt no fear, he knew every inch round there. Soon afterwards, the police cars were roaring past, blue lights flashing and sirens sounding. Rettenberger watched them go with an amused glance, then got on the bus, paid for the ticket to St Pölten with the last few coppers he had in his pocket and sat down on one of the middle seats. The bus was only lit up inside when it halted at a stop. He cruised along through the dusk on this ship of the country roads that stopped every few hundred metres, taking longer for the ten or so kilometres to St Pölten than for his two hold-ups put together, including the time it took him to get to and from the banks. He wouldn't have minded if the bus, which he used to hate because it was so slow, had taken much longer. As if that would allow him to catch up on the time he had rushed through so quickly during the hold-ups.

Two stops before the railway station in St Pölten, he got off, went to his own car, parked in the town hall square, and set off back for Vienna. Instead of taking the West Autobahn again, he followed the detour via Hainfeld, Alland and the Outer Ring Road. In Vienna he bought the evening papers, finding, as expected, only reports of the Creditanstalt robbery. When he got back home shortly after seven and his girlfriend asked him where he had been, he said, 'Out for a drive.' He looked so calm and contented she thought nothing of it and assumed he had been to St Leonhard, where he grew up, for a run, as he had several times recently.

Rettenberger spent the morning walking backwards and forwards along the ridge. He sucked in the sun-warmed air, as if that would rid him of the terrors of the bitterly cold night. He strode up and down his path tirelessly, patrolling, guarding his territory. Time and again he passed the signposts, of which he had only been able to decipher a fraction during the night. Near the shrine there was a large map of the whole area. He stood looking at it several times, per-using marked paths, the various shapes of the hills and mountains around, comparing them with his ridge and studying their names. The Anninger alone was cut up into so many hills and ridges on its west-ern flank that it was covered in names: the Broad Pine, the Hussars' Temple, the Witch's Seat, the Baby Matterhorn, the Dead Man, the Storm Cross and the Armchair. Every inch of the chain of hills from Mödling to Baden had writing on it, but for the moment that was of no use to him. First of all he had to get off this hill. However, he kept on just sitting there, looking around, towards Sittendorf, for example. That meant he had the autobahn right under his nose, but he made no attempt to get down there, as if by this time he had been hemmed in by his own walking up and down. He simply watched the cars drive past. As if pulled along by a hand, they drew lines, often only deviating from the others by millimetres, on the broad tarmac. Then he went back along the ridge.

From the Schwarzkopf, at the eastern end, he could look down on Gaaden, which seemed quiet, and on the road junction, where three police vehicles were drawn up. The policemen were standing beside them, like apathetic hitchhikers. Sometimes they stuck their hands in their pockets, sometimes they stretched their legs. They must find something to talk about all day, he thought, otherwise they couldn't stand being together. And he was astonished, as he was always astonished when he observed other people, at how much they did have to say to each other. If he could have avoid hitting the trees, he could have thrown pebbles down at them.

As Rettenberger turned away, he remembered that during the night he had dreamt he was standing at the edge of a mountain road, looking down a steep white slope. He is completely unaffected by the drop. The mountainside is smooth. As smooth and white as Carrara marble. The ideal place to commit suicide, is the thought that flashes through his mind. All he would have to do would be to jump and he would go shooting down the slope as if it were a children's slide. And he would die. Quickly Rettenberger erased all such thoughts from his mind, walked on a little way then sat down again in the sun.

Only when it was starting to get dark did awareness of his situation return. He stopped in his tracks, as if he had to bring not only himself, but all the walking and sitting to a standstill, the sitting and walking and looking around without seeing of the previous hours. For the first time he asked himself how he was going to get out of these woods. He had wasted a whole day when he ought to have been concerned with nothing else. Now, in the twilight, was the time when his pursuers would most expect him to try and break out.

There were a few more metres up to the Eichkogel at the western end of the ridge. He could hardly see the path. And the idea of spending another night up here frightened him. He turned round on the spot and headed back towards the Schwarzkopf. He wanted to know what the search parties were doing, whether they were still there, even if from that distance he could not learn much about how they were going about the search. Rettenberger sat down among the trees above the steep slope, ate the remaining sandwiches and watched the police officers below. He found it strangely reassuring that they were still there, standing in the same place. He was probably even more exhausted than in the morning, but his feverishness had gone. Now he knew what to do. The policemen wouldn't be able to stop him.

Cautiously he stood up, went back a little until he was among the trees, then worked his way down the slope, keeping an eye on the watchers at the junction, now illuminated by the street lamps. Soon he could see the gleam of the road to Gaaden below, hear the sound of the stream before it. It was steeper than it had looked here and he clung onto tree trunks. In the dark he could only progress slowly if he was not to lose his footing. He wanted to get down at least as far as the stream, so great was his thirst by now. He felt as if everything depended on getting that drink. As he cautiously continued his descent, his only thoughts were of the cool water, as if thinking could bring it to him. The sound of the stream was loud, the closer he came, the less he could hear of his own steps, he could no longer hear the cracking of twigs, the rustle of dry leaves, just occasionally he felt himself slip, everything else was drowned in the flow of the water.

When he reached the stream Rettenberger dipped both hands, like a shell, into the water and quickly bent his face over it, none of it must run out between his fingers, he drank it down thirstily. So far he had given no thought to the fact that he had to cross the stream. Given that there were policemen posted at the one bridge, the other bridges would be guarded too. The water was pitch black, so that he could not see how deep it was anywhere. Rettenberger walked along the bank. Eventually he lost patience, took off his shoes, socks and trousers and cautiously stepped in where he thought it might be shallow. At his first step the water hardly came up to his ankles, at his second also. But then it was slapping round his calves. It was icy cold, it was wonderful, and it did not get any deeper. Immediately his feet felt refreshed. On the other side he sat down, dried his feet on the lining of his leather jacket, got dressed and climbed up the slope to the road with a warm, tingling feeling in his shoes. Perhaps he was fortunate the street lighting was rather minimal, or the policemen happened to be looking the other way. Whichever it was, he crossed the road and nothing happened.

He felt a strange sense of anticipation as he approached the village from a distance. On the part of the high street he could see from the woods there was certainly plenty of bustle between the shops. It must have been shortly before six. In the country there was always a special atmosphere at that hour of the day, when the housewives were doing their last bit of shopping, the men coming home from work, especially in late autumn and winter when it was already dark and the light from the window displays, the street lamps and the car headlights cast a warm glow over the streets. He was familiar with it from St Leonhard. As a child he had always gone shopping at that time with his mother and some of his brothers and sisters. They rushed round the grocer's, to the post office, to the chemist's. All at top speed because the littlest children had been left at home alone. Enviously he watched other mothers who even – or perhaps especially – at that hour had time to stop for a chat out in the street or in the few shops. What a feeling of security that must give the other children, even more when their father came home from work. He imagined him stroking their hair with his rough hand, asking them what had happened at school, how they were getting on with their homework. He could not imagine life with a father in any greater detail. The only thing he could remember of his own father, who had disappeared from their family life so early on, was the stinging smell of cold cigarette smoke. His face, his voice he had forgotten, he didn't even know if he had liked him.

Rettenberger stood behind a tree watching a road that led to the nearby estate. Cars kept on turning off the main road into it, mostly mothers with children, only occasionally men. Then there would be shouts, warnings, front doors opening, light spilling out from hallways, doors closing again, lights being switched on in the houses, and silence would return. It didn't seem possible to get a car without being observed. But at least he could try his luck, take a turn or two round the estate, better just the one, otherwise people would be sure to notice him. When he was finally out of these woods, the right car was bound to turn up and he would get onto the autobahn, where it would be impossible to stop him, so quickly would he be gliding through the night. No witnesses, that was the important thing, or the police would be on his tail again immediately.

Rettenberger came away from his tree and slipped out of the woods. No one must see him as he covered those few yards through the trees. Once on the pavement people would take him, at least at first sight, for an ordinary pedestrian; if he was seen coming out of the woods, he was the bank robber.

Shortly before 6 pm Rettenberger left his hiding place. Martha A., 35, who runs a tobacconist's, found him lying in wait for her at her Anningerstrasse home in Gaaden when she arrived back from work. Pointing his gun at her, he demanded her car keys. Terrified, she handed them over. Then she was told she had to get into the boot as a hostage. She already had one foot in when a police patrol car happened to pass. Rettenberger fled into the woods, keeping the car keys, but without the car.

Even before the attempted car theft, witnesses claimed to have seen the escaped bank robber. A long-distance lorry-driver stopped in Berndorf, to the south of Gaaden, and told police he had seen Rettenberger on the road. In Sparbach empty houses were searched for clues, but nothing was found. In Böheimkirchen a traffic policeman shot at a van that ignored signals to stop. The driver was later caught; he had no driving licence. 19-year-old Manfred G. from Gaaden also came under fire. His windscreen was shattered when, due to a misunderstanding, he ignored a road block the police had set up. Superintendent Alfons Traninger, who was on the spot, said he hoped they would have more success in the hunt for Rettenberger that night.

The previous night they thought they had the wanted criminal surrounded. 500 police were deployed round an area of 50 square kilometres to the north of the Anninger. However, as we now know, Rettenberger managed to slip through the cordon.

When Rettenberger saw the patrol car he was so furious he felt like shooting the woman there and then. He had intended to take her with him and leave her tied up somewhere where he would be well away from his pursuers when they found her, so that anything she told them would not put the police back on his trail. But she had been so clumsy he hadn't quite managed to get her into the boot. The men in the patrol car had seen one of her legs. If she had been in the boot he would have simply closed it, got into the driver's seat and started the engine, just as if he had every right to be in the car. The officers were unlikely to have recognised him. They didn't even take a shot at him as he ran away. Perhaps he had given them more of a shock than they had him.

His annoyance at the botched kidnapping was good for his running. He came to a forestry track. If he remembered the area map correctly, it went up the Anninger. Even as he ran away from the estate he was already going at a pretty good pace. He had immediately fallen into an aggressive stride, which blotted out the memory of the incessant plodding to and fro of the previous day. Rettenberger was proud of how much strength he still had. The forestry track was steep, as if drawn with a ruler up the mountain side. He was running at the limit. He was fast, and he scarcely dared wonder how far he could keep going like that. His open leather jacket fluttered out like wings behind him; he had already unbuttoned his woollen cardigan. By now he had really got into his running and the pain he felt was necessary as resistance: as long as he concentrated on that, he didn't have to think of the climb facing him, the Anninger, the police or the night that was to come; he was running away from all that, an expression of grim determination on his face. All the way up he was running through the pain barrier they said you had to overcome around the thirty- or thirty-five-kilometre mark in a marathon. The others would have to overcome it too if they were going to catch him. Let them try.

Past the looming Schenkenberg, up the Buchtal and the narrow gully of the Steinwandl Graben: after a good quarter of an hour he had reached the Anninger Mountain Hut. At that pace the police had no chance. It would only have taken two or three minutes to send out a general alarm, but by the time they'd agreed on the direction to take, he was already half way up the mountain.

Rettenberger felt safe. He even enjoyed the view as, cautiously and keeping his distance, he ran past the hut, which was obviously closed. He tried to relax his leg muscles by adopting a slower tempo, but he mustn't stop, or he wouldn't be able to take another step. From here there was a road to Mödling. He could run down it, but it would be much too dangerous. If the police decided to cordon off the western flanks of the Anninger, that would be their main route up to the ridge. After he had run round the hut, he realised that he was keeping too close to the route he had literally flown up two days ago. Now he was running back down it. However, as long as he was so far ahead of his pursuers, the precise direction didn't matter. Before he set off down to Gumpold-skirchen and was swallowed up by the trees, Rettenberger had one last look at the distant lights of Vienna, single patches of light of different sizes, as if threaded along the thin line of the South Auto-bahn, whilst beyond them more night-dark fields stretched far away to the east, as if they were already waiting for him.

Rettenberger's girlfriend, Erika Borek, who has no criminal record herself, admitted she was the first to identify him as 'The Mask' when she saw the closed-circuit television pictures from the banks he had held up. 'What did I do wrong?' is the question she keeps asking, tormenting herself with reproaches while she is held on remand.

Erika got to know Rettenberger in the middle of 1984. At the end of February that year he had been released on parole. Later he moved in with her in her apartment in the Simmering district of Vienna. She was happy to share her flat with the 'likeable' young man, even though he was unemployed. She says she felt maternal towards him and he had promised not to rob any more banks.

After the end of the woods the path became a road going straight into Gumpoldskirchen. He was running without having to think about it now, but Rettenberger knew how deceptive such feelings were, knew that a fast ascent took its toll as soon as you were back on the flat, making your legs seize up so that you could hardly put one foot in front of the other. Before he reached the town he veered off into the vineyards.

A picture in the newspaper shows Rettenberger with his girlfriend after he had won the *Kainach Mountain Marathon, the toughest hill race in Austria. With a time of 3 hours 16 minutes he beat the master long-distance runner, Josef Hones, by four minutes to take the prize of 5,000 schillings. His girlfriend, Erika Borek, was there to cheer him on.*

In the photo Rettenberger looks almost happy. He is standing next to his girlfriend in a clean white singlet and his black running shorts. His eyes are shining, even though after his exertions they seem to be more deeply set. Rettenberger's legs go up well above the hips of the stocky woman; thin, wiry and much too long, they look as if they could not support even the slim upper body of a runner, but once set in motion, they would fly along. Oddly, the woman beside him is looking away, to one side; she is holding a kind of plate, a trophy she has clearly already taken possession of. Erika Borek has fairly short hair, dyed blond at the parting, and is wearing a white dress. In a way, standing next to Rettenberger she looks like a waitress.

Rettenberger crossed the railway line, the canal to Wiener Neustadt and the trunk road. Then he took to the fields. He had been looking forward to an uninterrupted run on the flat like this. For a while he followed the course of the River Schwechat, until it went under the autobahn, then kept to the western side of the motorway, heading north on his own little lane beside the broad carriageway, coming closer to Vienna, which was still some way away. More than anything else, at that point he needed the autobahn. The constant swish of vehicles passing, the regular sweep of the lights, the variety of engine noises all encouraged him not to stop, to keep running into the icy north wind, as if his legs did not know the meaning of tiredness.

Rettenberger had soon left Guntramsdorf behind

and managed to squeeze unseen past Wiener Neu-
dorf, where the houses reached almost right up to
the autobahn. At Maria Enzersdorf he ran round the
stadiums, sports halls and swimming pools of the
National Training Centre. Seeing the groups doing
their evening training on the running tracks, he
would like to have known what his own split times
were. He had probably been running for about
thirty-five minutes since Gumpoldskirchen, a good
time for the ten kilometres or so.

Farther ahead the lights of a town began, while to
the left the fields stretched almost as far as the main
road. Rettenberger thought about running on into the
city, but there was little point, since he had no idea
where he would find somewhere to spend the night in
Vienna. At the last fields by Maria Enzersdorf he
turned away from the autobahn and headed straight
for the houses.

Before he was sent to prison he had been crazy about
another woman. She was a year older than him, deli-
cate, fairylike. Perhaps, he sometimes thought later,
he had tried to rob the bank because of her, so that,
like some fairytale prince, he could whisk her away
from a life selling women's tights. But this had probably only occurred to him in retrospect; in time even
she would have become a woman like Erika for him.

With long strides Rettenberger ran across the freshly
ploughed field. The clods of earth were hard from the
cold, which stopped him from sinking in too far, but
also exposed him at every step he took to the danger

of losing his balance and falling, putting all his weight on his ankle. Immediately the ligaments would tear or snap. With an oddly loud noise – he was familiar with it from football – that reverberated, even though it came from inside the foot. As he continued to stride out confidently across the night-black ploughland, Rettenberger shivered, but more from the strange excitement thoughts of this kind gave him than from fear. The lights of the town hardly seemed to be getting nearer. There were no hills, no fences, no bushes he could use to orient himself. Even the autobahn was too far behind him to serve as a point of reference. It was more as if he were running into himself rather than to somewhere else, gradually disappearing out of the world with an expression of quiet pride on his face.

Prison had locked up his life, his whole life, locked away all his hopes. After his release he was a nobody, someone who no longer knew who he was himself. As a child he had often wished he could be someone else, now he could put on all sorts of masks without having to disguise himself. The Runner. The Boyfriend. The Robber. The Murderer. Yet what he most longed to be able to do was to disappear completely behind one of these masks, fuse with it. That was the sole reason why, after he came out of prison, he had been so successful as a runner. He kept extending his training runs more and more, did two, three, sometimes even four circuits of the Prater. He could not stop himself. He had to stay that long on his feet so that he could continue to hide behind the mask of The Runner in

the tiredness afterwards. And he felt the same pull as
The Robber. The automatic gestures during a hold-
up, the loud threats, the horrified faces made him see
himself so clearly as The Robber, that it was a sight
he became more and more greedy for.

Rettenberger had managed to hurry through Maria
Enzersdorf without attracting attention. The shops
had long since closed. The bright lights from their
windows illuminated empty space. No one was
around at this hour, they were having their dinner.
He had briefly wondered whether he ought to walk,
but he did not have the patience. Perhaps, he
thought, the people would not betray him to the
police, perhaps they felt sympathetic towards him,
were trembling a little, were keeping their fingers
crossed for him as they watched their televisions
while he was running through their towns, past their
cosy houses.

He did not even feel sadness when he thought of the
time before he was sent to prison. He could not
remember anything. The years of his childhood and
youth lay behind him, a dead life, all memory of it
had died a slow death in prison. There was anger in
him, but otherwise nothing remained. His anger was
like a sacred memento, he felt good in his anger.
When anything went wrong, the merest trifle, he
would start shouting; if he dropped something when
washing up, he would fling two or three more items
down to join it. At the same time his anger provided
a means of getting away from Erika's contented

understanding, her affection, which was threatening to envelop him more and more. She could not stand his unpredictable aggressive outbursts. She was frightened and fear turned her face grey, her expression almost cross.

After passing through the middle of the town he headed west again, out towards the hills above Giesshübl. The road up through Barmhartstal was straight as an arrow, almost going as far as the Outer Ring Autobahn. On either side were detached houses, all clearly belonging to small, well-off families and permanently occupied. He had a vague memory that there were summer houses here as well. He ran along in the wake of a faint hope. And he was not disappointed; here, as in the districts of Vienna that included sections of the Vienna Woods, the dwelling houses suddenly gave way to an estate of summer houses, almost identical in appearance and two-thirds the size. Not a single one had lights on. A hundred yards further on the road ended; high time he stopped. Hardly believing he could still stay on his feet, he hobbled over to one of the garden gates. All these places were obviously empty during the week. He had no problem getting into the house.

The robber is asleep. Sound asleep. Perhaps his hold-ups run through his dreaming mind, like a film, and he is the bold, proud Robber. But his favourite dream is not of carrying out the robbery but of putting the fear of God into those he is robbing. Then the bank robber is more The Hunter than The Robber. In his dream he terrifies everyone. He steals his way into the dreams of others, he is the only one who cannot be woken from his sleep in the middle of the night, quivering with fear. Thus the bank robber dreams his whole life, terrifying even the brightest of days.

THE DEATH OF THE ROBBER

The Wednesday paper is full of pieces on Johann Rettenberger. The banner headline on the front page is: *MASKED ROBBER INVESTED SPOILS ABROAD*. A large photo shows an armed-response unit storming a haybarn. Two members of the unit can be seen on the picture. One has all the special equipment: helmet, bullet-proof vest, powerful rifle; the other, behind him, bareheaded, with just a grey official-issue pullover, is clutching his pistol. Below are pictures of the three men Rettenberger encountered on the fourth day of his flight, and a photo of Rettenberger himself. He is staring into space, as is commonly the case with photographs of criminals.

On that Tuesday, as on every weekday, 57-year-old Friedrich Müller from Maria Enzersdorf, manager of a building supplies depot, got up at half past six and went to the tobacconist's to buy cigarettes and a newspaper. As he sat over his coffee, he wondered whether to start with the local news for once, given that the bank robber still had not been caught, but then turned to the sports pages after all. As always, his wife told him he ought to eat something. She said it merely out of habit, more or less speaking to herself. She didn't want to talk to him, on the contrary, she used it to keep him at a distance. He already had his cigarette in his hand and said, 'Yes, yes,' as he took his first puff. He had not the slightest intention of eating anything. Instead he read his newspaper, turned the page. He had the feeling she was staring at him all the time. The well-known phrases, which were all he heard from her, sounded more and more cynical. They echoed round inside his head, mocking him by the mere fact that they pretended to be directed at him. He leafed through the newspaper, from back to front, turned to the back pages again, read the *In Brief* items on the sports page and studied the league tables. Secretly he admired her staying power. Now that other women were not interested in him, she had ended up the winner.

Some time between half past seven and a quarter to eight Müller went down to get his car and drove the six kilometres to his office in Vösendorf. There he went through the paperwork that had been put out for him and the post. Otherwise there was nothing for him to do. He had been manager for five years and that was as far as he was going to get. He did not even have any children. He had never done any sport and it was far too late to think about doing something about his fitness out of vanity. As so often, he would knock off work a couple of hours early today, this time to get his summer-house ready for the winter. Actually there was no reason why he could not have gone there straight away. Life could be so nice, was one of his wife's sayings.

Every day the papers have more photos of the hunt for the bank robber. At the same time this accumulation of pictures of eye-witnesses, police cars, officers in action and lines of dogs more and more gives the impression of desperation. As if by publishing them they felt could get the escaped robber in their power. On the inside pages of the Tuesday paper there is another picture of a surrounded house, a tiny white house that looks ruinous and abandoned. Policemen have crept up and flattened themselves against the walls, their heads are on a level with the gutters, their rifles at the ready. Underneath it says: *Countless buildings were surrounded, stormed and searched – Rettenberger was nowhere to be found.*

Shortly before six on the Tuesday Josef Grafenecker, a retired railway worker who ran a small farm, was in the sty seeing to his pigs. Then he sat down in the kitchen, drank his coffee, ate some bread and butter, mopping up the last of his milky coffee with it, and listened to the radio.

At half past six his wife thumped on the banisters to wake their two children, who were at the high school. With each year that passed Grafenecker had less and less idea of what they were learning, but was sure they would end up with good jobs. He had only gradually come to terms with the thought that neither of them wanted to take over the farm. There would not be a place for him and his wife to stay there when they had to give up the farm. He did not look forward to going into an old folks' home, he refused to think about it. Grafenecker smiled. As always, the slightly whining moans of his children about the noise of the folk music from the radio would be the first he heard of them. They came into the kitchen, still half asleep, they hadn't said anything yet. Recently the older boy had started saying 'folksy music', which did nothing to reduce his dislike of it, on the contrary. 'Real folk music' wasn't bad, he said, but what his father listened to was 'the pits.' Before any protest could be made, Grafenecker switched the radio off and went to the bathroom. His children were strangers to him, but perhaps that was the way they had to be at their age.

The robber sleeps until the morning is well advanced. He looks calm as he does so, as if it will be a long time before he wakes up on this cold, wet Tuesday. The night's rain has turned into dense, murky fog hanging over the Vienna basin, with a strong wind blowing above it. The robber in his summer house by the hill above Giesshübl sees nothing of that, the nearby Outer Ring Autobahn goes roaring by and he lies there, coddled in the warmth of his stolen clothing. But if he were to open his eyes, he would have a wonderful view out over a landscape swathed in grey cotton wool. Accompanied by the swish of the cars that keeps mingling with the showers of rain, splashing up in whorls of spray and falling back to earth, like the white horses of a sea on the shores of which there is nothing to do but sleep, safe and sound.

Shortly before eight Inspector Andreas Hauer went to the police station in the town hall square in St Pölten. He had had Saturday to Monday off and had therefore only followed Rettenberger's escape in a private capacity. After the first setbacks he had not felt the urge, in contrast to other, similar large-scale operations, to ring his colleagues for details, so that all he knew was what he had learnt from the radio, television or newspapers.

As soon as he entered the duty room, he sensed the peculiar concentration that had them all in its grip. His colleagues gave him their usual greeting, but they hardly looked up from their files, newspapers or coffee cups. No one asked him how his weekend had been. After Hauer had hung up his jacket and sat down at his desk, Weinzettel continued to read aloud from the newspaper, as if he had not been interrupted by Hauer's entry: *'Once more the police are in danger of becoming a target for mockery. In the latest game of "cops and robbers" some cops have not exactly covered themselves in glory. For example, in order to create a "positive atmosphere," a highly dangerous murderer had his handcuffs removed in the dilapidated police station on Rennweg. And those guarding him were surprised that he took advantage of the opportunity with a daredevil leap out of the window! "It all happened so quickly, we weren't expecting it."* That's what he wrote,' said Weinzettl, his voice bitter with hatred, as if he would have liked to smash the journalist's face with his words. *'If there had been a slowness-on-the-uptake competition, it certainly would not have been Rettenberger who won it. According to a police spokesman, the reason for the pathetic lack of success in catching Rettenberger was that the bank robber was in "superb condition". Which others obviously are not.'*

When no one made any comment, Weinzettl went on, *'Our officers would be well advised to bring all their muscles up to the same level of fitness as their fingers, which are clearly world class from their years of writing out parking tickets.'*

'Bastard,' said one of the younger policemen, who had just come off patrol. Otherwise nothing was said, they all, Hauer included, returned to their files. As long as there was no report of a successful outcome to the pursuit, as long as they did not even know where Rettenberger was, they could do nothing but sit there twiddling their thumbs. Cursing or flying into a rage would be just a futile expression of impotence.

At half past two they were called into action. Rettenberger had been seen in a stolen car on the Outer Ring Autobahn. Hauer and his colleagues were ordered to the West Autobahn to set up a road block before the St Pölten South exit. They rushed there, blue lights flashing, stopped all the traffic in both lanes, put in place the barriers that could be dropped across the carriageway, then the cars were roaring past again. During recent operations on the autobahn Hauer had often felt afraid, unable to stop himself imagining that a driver not paying attention, or even unconscious from a heart attack or a stroke, might drive straight into them. In the meantime more and more reports of sightings of Rettenberger were coming in: He was in Böheimkirchen; patrol cars were following him near St Christophen; he had turned off the autobahn; he was driving back towards Vienna. Every radio report put Rettenberger in a different place, as if he were constantly changing course, popping up now here, now there on the autobahn in his seven-league boots. They stood there by their cars like dolls, with no idea where Rettenberger actually was at the moment. Perhaps he had long since driven past, waving, and they had not seen him.

At last, after three o'clock, there came more and more radio messages that Rettenberger was heading towards them. When he actually appeared at the start of the long straight, with the helicopter above and the long tail of police cars behind him, they finally had their chance to show what they could do. Each man was in place, as far as possible in cover. Then it all happened quickly, as it does in that kind of operation when suddenly every action is automatic, when experience takes over from excitement. They all had their guns trained on the car hurtling towards them, then the mesh barriers were torn apart, flew through the air, hitting the posts, the police vehicles, over their heads and into the ditch behind them.

Rettenberger had simply driven straight through. No one had fired a shot. They had watched him, as if paralysed, keeping their heads down. Hauer gave the door of his car a kick, Rettenberger was speeding away up the rise. Hauer swung round with his gun and, blind with rage and with no hope of stopping Rettenberger, emptied the whole magazine in the direction of the car that roared on and disappeared from view over the hill, as if guided by an invisible hand.

One of the photos published on the Wednesday just shows a dead figure. Rettenberger is wearing a thin pullover and jeans. His body is slumped, his right hand between his legs, his thumb touching his crooked index finger. The driver's door has been opened and his left arm is hanging out, dangling down from the body lying on its side. What this picture records is not just a death, but the first viewing, the look to ascertain that the bank robber is dead. His head is in the centre of the photo, though his face cannot be seen, only his hair, a little whorl on the crown of his head and, farther forward, odd strands sticking up in one or two places, as if he had just brushed his hair back with his hand. A last sign of life in a newspaper photo which otherwise, with the car around him, looks like a death mask.

It is quite late when Rettenberger wakes up on the Tuesday. His body has greedily sucked in the sleep he needs and that is why, when he first wakes up, he feels dazed. He lies still in the television chair with its back lowered until he notices that his body, damp with sweat from the night, is steaming in the cold of the summer-house. He looks at the ceiling. He has the feeling that only now is the pressure of the last few days being relieved. All the agitation, all the exertions are dissolving into thin air and in this cold he can even see it happening.

Rettenberger stays lying there, without moving, until he feels himself start to shiver. While his body is still warm, his sweat is slowly cooling. He wishes his clothes would just lift an inch or two so that he could slip out of them without having to touch them. But soon the cold has spread all over his body. He gets up and goes into the tiny bathroom. He has to force himself to take a shower, but then realises how necessary it was, he feels so light and new. Now they could make a TV advert with him, he thinks, soft-focused pictures of The Robber, with Cat Stevens's 'Morning has broken' in the background, breakfasting on a terrace looking out over sunlit parkland and drinking his tea from fine bone China like a young lord.

Rettenberger puts on a dressing gown and sits down at the kitchen table. Out of the window he watches the mist lying over the flat land of the Vienna basin. The fine day yesterday was clearly an aberration on the part of the weather. He gets up and looks through various drawers and cupboards for some different clothes, finally, right at the back of one, finding a pullover and trousers that look as if they were made for him. Probably belonging to the owner's son. The jeans are tight round his hips, the slight stretch means the material covers him like a second skin. And while he is aware of the elastic embrace of the pullover, the trouser legs widen below the knees so that he can hardly feel them, as if they were flying round his calves.

Rettenberger wonders whether Erika could imagine that this time he is not coming back. He assumes that once she is released from remand she will soon find someone else. The next man on his stumbling way through life will surely fall straight into her open arms, not radiant with joy, but relieved at his good fortune. Perhaps after all there had been moments when he loved her. For example the day when she realised he was a bank robber. For a few moments she had lost her self-belief, her tears had shown at least a trace of helplessness. Only at such times had he had enough strength for an emotion like love.

He goes to sit at the window again with a glass of water. He has no idea what time it is, has not seen a clock here, not even an alarm clock. It must be late morning. In some of the gardens he sees rakes and spades leaning against the sheds, but nowhere are there signs that any of the summer houses is occupied. For the moment he feels safe, has enough time to think about how he is going to get away from here without being noticed. His new clothes give him a feeling of lightness. As on Saturday evening when he floated past the two policemen and out of the window like a feather. He still needs to find a suitable jacket. Shoes he has already seen, white tennis shoes which simply have to be the right size.

By the early afternoon he is still wondering how to get hold of a car out here. One of the main reasons why the complex of summer houses is so quiet is that not a single car has appeared. He does not get any further with his plans when he considers the detached houses and bungalows back along the road. He must not lose his nerve now. He needs the afternoon to rest. It gets dark between five and six. Then he could go down the Barmhartsthal road in the dark, like someone taking a short walk over the hill before dinner. In that way he would get to Maria Enzersdorf just before the shops closed, when there was sure to be someone in enough of a hurry to leave the key in the ignition outside one of the grocers. Rettenberger imagines himself driving the few kilometres north to Brunn am Gebirge, where he would have two motor-ways to choose from, one going south, one going west. He wonders which one he will take, weighs the pros and cons. In fact, though, it is no contest, so strong is his urge to head westwards.

While he is thinking this over, he hears a car approaching. At first it does not interrupt his train of thought, since the noise fits in perfectly with his plans. Then it does jolt him out of his pondering. There is an Audi parked by the fence. Not seeing anyone, he initially assumes the owner of his summer house must be at the door, but then he sees the man in the neighbouring garden. A tall, heavy-looking figure wearing a hat and coat. Rettenberger watches him go into the house, come out minus his coat and look round, spending far too long staring at the next-door house, as if he knows full well who is there. Then he starts working on the lawn with his rake. Why did he stare like that? is the question going round and round in Rettenberger's head. The man couldn't have seen him; if he had the police would be there in no time at all. Rettenberger cannot make up his mind about it, while the man calmly goes on working in his garden, not much more than three metres away from him. He sits down at the table, tries to put it out of his mind. Then he looks out of the window again and all at once he knows what is to be done. He puts the tennis shoes on, they are a perfect fit, takes the gun, opens the back door as quietly as possible and creeps out of the garden on tiptoe. He must have looked really funny, he thinks later, when he is in the car. Like an actor rehearsing the part of an amateur robber for an English film. Rettenberger hides behind the large Audi, though the man is concentrating so hard on what he is doing, he would not have needed to hide at all. He opens the garden gate, goes up to him from behind and sticks the gun in his back, saying, 'Don't shout.' The man slowly straightens up and drops the rake straight away. Rettenberger can tell from the man's thickest body what an effort he has to make to keep on breathing out and in. It is a long time before his first breath comes.

Rettenberger gives him time, just gently urging the man, who is taking deep breaths, out of the garden gate, walking beside him like a son supporting him, until he gets him in the other summer house. There he makes him sit down, takes off his trousers and shoes and ties him to the chair with the trousers and a tablecloth. He senses the man, who is still gasping for breath, knows who he is. Rettenberger also takes his hat and glasses, he might need them as a disguise, he has already found the car keys in the pocket of his trousers. He leaves the man, who clearly still cannot believe this is happening to him, sitting in the chair, and goes out to the car. He has solved a big problem at a stroke.

A few seconds later Rettenberger already has the car in second gear, driving down through Barmhartstal. It has started to rain as he drives past the detached houses, all fenced round like little castles. Presumably the man in the summer house also owns one of these mini castles somewhere. Now he's sitting up there all alone, probably still gasping for breath, experiencing the biggest adventure in his whole life.

Rettenberger drives back into Maria Enzersdorf. As he turns left by the church, he reduces the setting of the windscreen wipers. The windscreen is immediately covered with a thick film of water, effectively screening him from view by the pedestrians, motorists and police in the town. He'd like to play some music on the car radio, American music for driving to, but it's still too early for that. On the main road from Maria Enzersdorf to neighbouring Brunn am Gebirge he has to stop several times in queues of vehicles waiting at red lights, now absorbed into the calm flow of the afternoon traffic. Rettenberger is counting on the police still being occupied with keeping the area to the north of the Anninger cordoned off, round the Little Anninger, the Witch's Seat and the Baby Matterhorn, possibly even round the Dead Man, waiting for him to appear out of the woods. And he is in the car, in the pouring rain, heading for the autobahn, with the heating on, the window wound down a fraction. In a gentle airstream he drives past factories and company headquarters, which are scattered all over the countryside along the road here and which, in a way, remind him of prisons, until he reaches the loops and curves of the autobahn junction.

Vienna, Budapest, Prague, all blind alleys for him, Graz, Ljubljana, Salzburg. He really has no other choice but to head for the West Autobahn. As the rain slackens off, Rettenberger glides along the various slip roads, past various signs, as if on the crest of a wave which builds up, through the looping threads of the cloverleaf, into a powerful breaker that pours onto the Outer Ring Autobahn. He needs to get out past St Pölten, Melk and Amstetten to the wide, flat countryside round Linz. That would be the first step, he refuses to think beyond Linz for the moment. In Linz he could have some music on. Rettenberger sends the car round the last loop. It responds well, that is clear from these first curves. The rain has stopped. He doesn't need it any more, doesn't want to have to take account of a wet road surface, accelerates onto the motorway, moves into the outside lane. The road begins to rise as it approaches the hills by Giesshübl, pulling Rettenberger up them.

Hardly had Rettenberger driven off in the green Audi 100, than Müller began to pull at his restraints. After ten minutes he managed to get hold of a kitchen knife and slice through the loosened bonds. In underpants and socks, still carrying the knife, he ran down to the nearest house, giving the woman, who was just coming out of the door with her child, the shock of her life. Close to a heart attack, he explained what had happened to him. The woman informed the police and the hunt began. Without that call, Rettenberger would have had enough of a start to escape again.

To overtake the first car Rettenberger applies minimal pressure to the accelerator, moves into the outside lane and already he is past it. He signals again, pulls in, continues at the same speed on the inside lane, catches up with the next car, accelerates, overtakes and pulls in again, enjoying the effortlessness with which he leaves everyone behind him as he drives along smoothly. There has only been a spattering of rain over the hills, the higher he gets, the drier the road surface becomes. Rettenberger overtakes one car after the other, signalling, pulling out, passing, signalling, pulling back into the inside lane in quicker and quicker succession.

From half way up the rise he stays in the outside lane so that he can easily maintain his speed, even when the gradient becomes steeper. Rettenberger knows this stretch of the autobahn well, always admires the view of the houses in Giesshübl as he drives up the hill; coming in the opposite direction, by day he loves the changing views of Vienna, by night the way the lights suddenly appear. Whilst the approach from the west makes Vienna look like a largish mountain town, from here, from the south-west, the whole spread of the city opens out.

At some point the summer houses in Barmhartstal must flit past, but by then he is no longer looking, he is concentrating on his line up the hill, aiming at the bridge carrying the road to Giesshübl across the autobahn at the top as if it were a decisive breakthrough point. If he had grown up here, he thinks, as a child he would certainly have spent as much time as possible sitting on the pavement of the bridge, dangling his legs through the bars of the fence above the car-roofs, enjoying the view of Vienna.

His car feels light as a feather as it takes the hill, so light that it forges ahead apparently unaware of its own weight. For a brief second, just before the summit, Rettenberger is overcome with a feeling of liberation, as if he had run up the whole way, had simply swept over the hill, becoming invisible to all his pursuers. And indeed, the next moment the view of the plain round Vienna and the grey of the city has disappeared from the rear-view mirror. The autobahn descends into the gentle slopes of the Vienna Woods, those rounded, pine-covered hills which, in contrast to other deciduous or mixed woodlands, recall southern landscapes.

Now the escaped bank robber and murderer, Johann Rettenberger, 30, will be standing before the Throne of Judgment. He was beginning to get a name for himself as the 'lonely fugitive,' On the TV news they called him 'Superman,' either from the toughest competition in the world or because of the 'Superman' television series. Or perhaps simply because 'super' is the favourite word of the poor in language.

You could already hear people saying, 'Can he run! He's a real athlete!' in a strange mixture of anger at the police's failure to catch him and admiration for the fugitive from justice.

Once he robbed three banks in one day, 'because things were going so well, not because I needed the money.'

What is it that makes a man who, on the outside, seemed so normal, into a murderer? Is it genetic, a congenital defect, like a short leg? That is something for the Supreme Judge to decide.

Rettenberger drives at high speed along the sweeping uphill and downhill curves of the Outer Ring Autobahn. It is simply impossible for him to drive more slowly, so painful is the longing he feels finally to get away from his pursuers. He holds the accelerator permanently two-thirds down, puts on just a touch more pressure to maintain his speed on the uphill stretches, and accelerates over the summits, before slackening the pressure of his foot on the downhill sections. Yet he still gets faster with each climb.

It is very satisfying, after having ended up surrounded each time he was literally on the run, to be flying along, heading straight for the horizon, at great speed. In the right-hand lane he leaves the line of cars he has overtaken behind him, to his left the crash barriers and low bushes of the central reservation flash past. He feels a lightness, an eagerness drawing him forward with a never-ending pull, which running, with the inescapable onset of tiredness, always eventually denied him.

One sweeping curve has taken Rettenberger past Sparbach and Sittendorf, left the Eichkogel and the Schwarzkopf disappearing in the distance. He does not even give them a glance. The car sticks firmly to the road, Rettenberger crosses the next hill, on the descent he is looking down on Alland, where he was on the first night of his escape. The next section is a valley with long curves until, on the western edge of the Vienna Woods, the autobahn starts to climb again. Rettenberger keeps his foot down on the accelerator. The car is powerful enough to make light of this stretch too, but then he hears a dull noise he knows, though he cannot see anything. He looks in the rear-view mirror, gripping the steering wheel as tight as he can, as if that will give him a better view, keeps looking in all directions, but can still only hear the throbbing noise above him. Finally he decides it must be a helicopter. He puts his foot down harder, going faster and faster until he reaches the top of the climb at Hochstrass and plunges into the rain, which returns with huge, splattering drops. He knows he cannot carry on like this for long. The first police cars, guided by the helicopter, will be waiting at the next exit, or the one after. The rain gets heavier. He keeps up his speed, as the road is still relatively dry, hoping to get through the shower, but gradually he starts to hear the swish of water under the tyres and he brakes as he comes down towards the next exit, though still overtaking all the other cars. Now he can see the helicopter flying along in front of him.

From the moment he hears the dull beat of the helicopter, in his mind's eye Rettenberger sees Kollhammer's face covered in pellet wounds again. His protruding eyes, his moustache, his cynical expression before everything disintegrated, his eyes burst, he literally cried his eyes out and they mixed with his blood, in which his moustache disappeared as well. At one blow Kollhammer had been torn apart before him.

His final feeling was one of satisfaction, even though it had shocked him that in the preceding moment he had suddenly perceived Kollhammer's expression as childlike. Now, particularly in view of that ultimately spurious innocence, he feels above all how necessary the shot was. Of those on the business finance course, Kollhammer was the undisputed king. The others believed all his stories implicitly. And Kollhammer talked all the time. He talked when someone else was talking, he talked during the classes, he talked during break. He was loud and smelt of sweat. Often he also smelt of semen as well. He mocked the few who took the course seriously, upbraided them. For the others Kollhammer was the strong Robber. They stared at him, wide-eyed, laughed out loud, ate out of his hand, so to speak, when he talked of brothels and whores, of card games and whisky, while in reality he was nothing but an ordinary husband and father. Perhaps they were impressed by the fact that, just like them he had a wife and child, but ignored them completely.

In the few weeks they had attended the retraining course together, Kollhammer had managed to snatch away the freedom Rettenberger had only just regained. He very quickly discovered that he could do as he liked with him, the former convict. While in prison Rettenberger had sometimes imagined that, as a bank robber, people outside would perhaps even treat him with something like awe, but here he was imprisoned again, helpless. And when during the breaks Kollhammer started blowing cigarette smoke in his face at every opportunity, he immediately knew he could not put up with it for long and blasted his face away a few days later.

Soon the autobahn will be completely wet, the long

channels made by the wheel-tracks filled with water. The helicopter is hovering in the air in front. In a way it is already a familiar sight. Still no patrol cars to be seen behind him; that will change, but until then there is nothing to be feared from the helicopter. Rettenberger turns off into the exit road, brakes, has difficulty holding the car, that is still going too fast, on the wet surface of the slip road, but it is only when he reaches the curve that he feels the full force of its momentum, pushing him towards the edge of the carriageway. For the first time since he set off in this car, he feels afraid, has no idea where to go. When he reaches the junction, he makes a spur-of-the-moment decision, does a U-turn and drives up the exit road and, with a shiver of excitement, shoots onto the wrong side of the autobahn, against the stream of traffic heading for Vienna.

Rettenberger pushes the car to its limit through the spray. The faster the oncoming cars come hurtling towards him, the less dangerous his driving seems to him. There is no more than a metre and a half between him and the safety barrier, probably only a metre to the edge of the road surface. Rettenberger is tearing along in a cloud of spray, the oncoming cars making his speed seem even greater, so that he sees the others as no more than shadows. His legs have gone numb, all he feels is that his right foot, pushing the accelerator down to the floor, will be the first thing to break should he actually crash into one these cars whose drivers, thunderstruck, jerk the steering wheel over and still only manage to get out of the way just before a collision. He is bare of emotion, no fear, no tension, just a strange calmness. If, as people sometimes say, drowning is a beautiful death, then he is drowning in his speed. He literally aims the car at those coming towards him and the more determined his aim, it seems, the quicker they take evasive action and the less he has to fear them.

As a child he always kept out of the way of the others. During break, before school, after school. He always tried to get past them, staying as invisible as possible. In the morning he would stop at the corner by the tennis courts and wait until the groups outside the school building had dispersed, swallowed up in the entrance, then quickly run the few hundred yards to slip into the classroom in time for the lesson.

What he most feared was the end of school each day. He always tried to be the first or the last. As soon as he was out of sight, he was off running. He slung his satchel over his shoulder, holding the strap tight, then stuck his hands out from his body, as if by doing that he could get himself freedom to move, at least space to breathe as he ran fast, with his school things still bumping up and down on his back. He knew the exact speed he could run at carrying the weight of his satchel, so that he could keep it up all the way home. He never had to stop, always kept running. Although he was getting away from others, this home run was a game that was his alone. Later he sometimes asked himself whether the inhabitants of the little town had ever wondered why this child ran home with his satchel on his back every day.

Perhaps the pilot cannot bring himself to watch him tearing along against the flow of traffic. Rettenberger seems to have shaken him off. He roars past Altlengbach, the rain coming at him horizontally. Despite the frantic efforts of the wiper blades, the windscreen is covered in a watery film. The tracks of the cars can hardly be seen on the road. When he hits water, it drags at the wheels, just holding him back before the surface tension of the water can suddenly assert itself and send him aquaplaning at uncontrollable speed into the first car to get in his way. He happens to look at the instrument panel and sees how low on petrol he is. But he cannot see the autobahn exits in time, the signs are not arranged for motorists going in the wrong direction. As far as Altlengbach the autobahn was straight, now he is driving into blind curves. It all goes so smoothly, he cannot even feel his foot any more, he hurls himself into them, flings himself at the oncoming cars as if they were waves pouring towards him in flurries of soft foam, only to disappear just before impact, just before they break in a scatter of spindrift, leaving him hanging in the void of the next leap into the next wave.

Only later, when he was already in training, did the locals start to observe him running. He clearly saw that they noticed him now, watched him disappear down the street, shaking their heads but impressed all the same. And those same schoolmates he had been so afraid of needed him for their football team. When they got to fourteen or fifteen a lot of them had stopped playing, so they needed him for the midfield, where all his running made sense to them. Now he was running with those he used to run away from, chasing the ball, which he got a thousand times more often than they did, and each time that was a triumph. And he won those early long-distance runs as well. His running was not running away any more, it was a chance to celebrate victories in front of all the others.

From the number of signs that appear in the slackening rain, Rettenberger eventually realises he is approaching the St Christophen exit. Not long before, the helicopter had reappeared behind him. The pilot would have been able to recognise him from a long way off as he forces his way through the oncoming traffic. When he visualises this, he feels proud for a moment. Then the backs of the signs begin to appear, probably with the distances to Vienna, the next service station, the next exit. How far will it be from here? How far after the slip road onto the autobahn are these signs normally positioned? He concentrates on a gap in the oncoming traffic that appears at the end of the next curve. It is not clear whether that will get him to the exit. All he can see is the gap. After the last car has shot past, with a short, sharp intake of breath he pulls the car across the other lane onto the hard shoulder, brakes as hard as he can and, seeing from the road markings in front that it is the exit, feels like shouting out loud. In a fit of pure joy he swings the car round hard, corrects the skid with a short burst of acceleration into the exit curve and drives on as if he had been coming from the right direction all along.

As he went up to Kollhammer's apartment, all he felt was a calm certainty. He did not creep along in the dark, he had switched the light on. He held the gun in his right hand. A few times it tapped on the steps like a walking stick. He checked the nameplates on the doors, even though he knew where Kollhammer lived, reading out the names, as if they were indications of what was hidden behind the doors.

Kollhammer lived on the third floor. From the gaps round the door it was clear there was no light on. Rettenberger rang the bell. Nothing happened. He rang again. He knew that Kollhammer would come to the door himself. He thought he knew everything about Kollhammer, his whole life was laid out before him, oppressing him, an exaggerated compilation of his boastful stories which had merged into a crazy caricature. He heard the steps, the door opening. Then he shot Kollhammer in the face, right in the look of astonishment on his face, turned round and went down the stairs. Outside he really felt like laughing out loud.

Of course, Rettenberger thinks, it could be that the helicopter pilot relaxed his attention for a moment or had perhaps become so accustomed to watching him drive towards all the oncoming cars, that he had actually allowed Rettenberger to escape. But, although as he drives away from the autobahn he cannot hear the sound of the rotors any more, he does not believe that. Instead he imagines that the pilot, quietly amazed at his manoeuvre, has flown in the wrong direction for a few seconds. Rettenberger brakes, slowly bringing down his speed. The tension is still there, but he feels calmer now. So far he has done everything right and he will continue to do everything right.

After the junction Rettenberger drives along for a while until he comes to some woods. Right, now it's your turn again, he thinks, referring to the helicopter pilot, whom he still cannot hear, though he senses his presence. He pulls up at the side of the road, leaves the hat, glasses and coat in the car and slips away into the trees. Even if the helicopter pilot does see the car in the thin cutting the road makes through the forest, Rettenberger will be invisible for a while among the dense conifers. Inside his head is he is still hurtling along, his whole body throbbing with the sensation of driving, and as he takes his first few steps he can even feel in his legs the effort of holding the accelerator down. The carpet of needles on the path softens the impact on his feet. And with every stride he shakes off a little more of the tension. It's the silence that makes running in the forest magical. The white tennis shoes feel not only light, but as soft as running shoes. He'd love to be going barefoot. At each step he can feel once more the gentle displacement of the pressure as the motion passes over the ball of his foot, and the single powerful thrust from the ankle joint that sends the forefoot springing up from the ground and into the next stride.

Now he feels a longing that is new to him. For the

first time he has the feeling he is coming close to somewhere where he is at home. In contrast to his running at other times, he has the definite impression he is heading in a particular direction. For the first time it is something more than simply his own movement, his hopes do not gradually reveal themselves as unattainable. He knows now where he wants to go, at last he is not running away any more.

Rettenberger feels secure. This longing envelops him like a protective film, wraps itself firmly round his skin, his hair, so that it seems that even running slowly he could soon take off and fly, or at least start to sing. Perhaps it is while smoothly jogging along like this that he falls into the light-footed step with which he eventually shoots out of the woods. Whilst he assumed, among all the tree trunks, that he was only making slow progress, out of the woods it is suddenly impossible to mistake how quickly he is going.

Josef Grafenecker, 56, left his Golf, registration number N 577.815, briefly outside his farm with the key in the ignition. He just popped into the barn, as he later told us, to fetch a pickaxe for some men working on the road outside. When he came back, his car had gone. 'I thought I must be seeing things,' he said, 'it was there a moment ago.' The roadworkers and a woman living nearby told him what had happened. A young jogger had casually run down the slope by the farm and driven off in the car. It was Rettenberger.

Spread out before him are meadows and ploughed

fields. The first farm is quite near, there are two others farther away, the village beyond them. Rettenberger has leapt into a peaceful scene which is so oblivious to anything outside itself that it does not react to this irruption. Beside the farm there are several workers round a hole in the road. There seems to be no one at the farm itself. Compared to the swiftness that now informs each of his strides, everything around seems to move at a slightly slower pace. As he heads across the fields towards the farm, he senses what the workers' next move will be before they make it. They straighten up, putting their hands on their hips as if they could not continue, and look at each other. The farmer comes out of his shed holding some tool or other. Rettenberger is only a few steps away from the little white car in the farmyard. No one would have an earthly chance of stopping him here. The key is in the ignition. That is what he assumed. In farmyards the keys are always left in the ignition, just as they are in city car parks where the cars are parked for you. Rettenberger slams the door shut, starts the engine and roars off along the country road beside the farm, watching the workers and the farmer in his rear-view mirror. They still have not shown any reaction.

Rettenberger feels he should rejoice, but for the moment the bumpy, switchback road is much too narrow. He hardly manages to get round the curves, several times he swerves, even on the straight stretches. The narrow road keeps disappearing, as if it were playing hide and seek, over blind summits and behind unexpected bends. Rettenberger drives on between ploughed fields and brown, autumnal meadows. Not even the most awkward country road is going to stop him, for he is certain this will take him to the autobahn slip road, where he will immediately be sucked back into the smooth flow of forward motion he loves so much.

As Rettenberger drives onto the autobahn he finds himself in the middle of a large number of police vehicles. Everywhere there are small white cars with blue flashing lights, in front of him, behind him, in the outside lane, all driving much more furiously than he is. At first Rettenberger stays in the inside lane, astonished at the chaos. The police seem to be concentrating so much on the hunt they do not recognise him, Rettenberger can have a good look at what is going on all round. He gets into lane, performing the manoeuvre in such a correct manner that the moment he appears in the pursuing vehicles, he disappears among them.

From being the quarry, Rettenberger has become one of his own hunters. Just like the policemen, he drives along doggedly after the bank robber, observing both them and himself as he does so. And just as when he was in the meadows outside the farm, it is as if simply by looking he slows down all other movement. Even the flashing blue lights no longer swirl, no longer flicker haphazardly over the surrounding area, as they usually do in the vicinity of any police car. Instead, they submerge in his astonished gaze, taking with them the aggression of such hunts. In complete contrast to when he came running out of the woods, he does not burst, light-footed and yet invisible, straight through the clutch of this slow motion, but remains clearly enclosed within it, as long as he just stays hidden. The rain has long since stopped. As it dries, the road surface becomes quieter and quieter, with only the hiss of the damp, misty air as they drive through it. Rettenberger is stuck in the pack of his pursuers. Just as in a film made in the studio, the landscape rolls past him, a backdrop, nothing more.

Eventually Rettenberger cannot stand driving along quietly any more. Nobody can hide for ever. Only a nobody can hide for ever – he senses that before he can say it to himself, so quickly is he swallowed up in the uniform flow. He puts his foot down again, he can hardly bear to stay under cover of this slow-motion world a moment longer. With the first car he stole instant acceleration would have been far easier. As it is, he has to build up momentum before he reaches the speed necessary to pull out into the outside lane. Rettenberger forces his way past the car in front and picks up enough speed on the next downhill to breathe a sigh of relief at the re-establishment of the speed differential, while the car's lack of power the uphill stretches reveal sends him into a fury of despair.

Eventually, however, Rettenberger gets to the front of the field and falls once more into his no-holds-barred tempo. For long stretches the autobahn is empty in front of him. Some drivers, obviously warned about the chase, have pulled up on the hard shoulder, others have parked in the picnic areas and are spectating from there. All that is lacking is the

first rays of the morning sun or a rainbow in the sky
in front of him. He merges with the road; he is not
flying yet, rather he is surging along on the crest of
a wave, a wave that is gradually building up. This is a
freedom no one is going to take away from him.

As on every other weekday, on 21 March 1988, a
Monday, the cars were beating their tattoo on
the irregular tarmac of Krottenbachstrasse. While
drivers heading into the city still retained their
momentum from the curving descent out of the
Vienna Woods, letting their cars more or less free-
wheel down this long straight before the traffic forced
them to slow down, all those going in the opposite
direction were desperate to get out of the city, seemed
to put their foot down automatically, so that Krottenbachstrasse always looked as if the cars were driving away from it. Even the pedestrians, exclusively
old people, found themselves drawn into the same
urgency, crossing the road to get to the park opposite
the branch of the Länderbank quickly, or hurrying
down the street to the station on the suburban line.
Krottenbachstrasse was always deserted. The only
people standing around there were delivery men,
people who did not know the district and tourists
asking the way.

Shortly before ten Rettenberger went into the
bank. As he did so, for the very first time he had the
feeling it might be his last hold-up. He could sense
every movement of his muscles, every flicker of his
eyelids, since getting out of the car he had observed
each and every one of his own actions, as if they

were following some predetermined scenario. It was all so familiar: the steps, the stone flags outside the glass doors, the metal grille to catch the gravel off the customers' shoes before they went into the bank, the sticker on the door with the times of opening and the one with the dog telling other dogs they were to stay outside. In his steps, his gestures, he was following the script laid down by the sequence of car door, pavement, bank entrance, following it almost blindly, as if he were at his own front door. Most banks had a kind of linoleum on the floor which clung to the soles of your shoes, slowing down your steps so that you proceeded at a measured, dignified pace. Would that make too brisk or clumsy robbers fall flat on their faces as they stormed in? Ignoring this question, he pulled his mask down over his face. What he dreaded at that moment, though, was the others' terror. In his mind's eye he could already see the expressions on their faces and they filled him with disgust. He did not want to have to see this fear, which paralysed him. What he would most have liked would have been for those around to put on masks too, while the hold-up took place.

The gun, the people, and the silence into which, as always, Rettenberger put his demand. The precise formulation did not matter. With the shotgun in his hand, he probably did not even need to express it in words. In that moment he was great, untouchable. As soon as the bag was filled and he had turned round, however, that all changed. Even if he still terrified the people, he was already on the run, a tiny figure, disappearing into the distance.

Rettenberger drives along the autobahn at the highest speed his car can manage, but it is still not flying. Rather it is a determined bid to free himself, cramped by the wish for greater speed. Rettenberger pushes the accelerator down to the floor, everything else is up to the engine, the gradient, even the wind. But the air itself seems to have clotted, everything around is blurred in the hazy light of the bank of thin cloud; a calm, mute timelessness which will never turn into a following wind.

Presumably, despite the terror he had spread with his hold-ups and all the things the newspapers had said about him, he would at some point or other have merged into the everyday world. Even bank robberies are part of normality, for which the only adjective that occurs to him is 'dreary'. A good November word. Perhaps it is finally to escape from his lifelong fear of disappearing that he now insists on staying at the head of the pursuit. He forces his way into the stretch ahead, pulling his pursuers along behind.

Rettenberger is no longer staring, spellbound, at the road quite so much; his attempts to swallow up all the distance separating him from the world outside do not make him go any faster. He looks ahead, into thin air – there is no horizon to speak of – and keeps driving. You never know, with time the car might find it easier too and will surpass itself. His arms, which have been braced against the steering wheel, relax, as does his leg, which has been pressing the accelerator so desperately against the restrictions of the car interior.

His pursuers fall into line in the rear-view mirror.

He wishes he could leave a choppy wake on the road behind him, like a boat hurtling along out of control, unexpectedly bringing disruption to those pursuing him. The police cars keep overtaking each other, clearly still trying to establish some order in the chase. As long as he is out in front of them, he is not afraid. On the contrary, he is relishing it now that he has established a clear lead over the rest of the field. He wouldn't, however, be surprised if the engine should suddenly start to judder and groan, leaving him no other option but to pull up at the edge of the road, on the hard shoulder, in the middle of the numerous onlookers who have already gathered, and, given the malfunctioning engine, quietly let himself be taken by his pursuers. But before that happens he is going to enjoy driving. He thinks of St Pölten ahead, of his proud, unbraking plunge into the flat land beyond, seeing himself pass by Ober-Grafendorf, Markersdorf, even St Leonhard am Forst.

Riding the wave of memory, the bank robber surged on through a world without motion. His breathing and heartbeat were already carried on the waves as they rose higher and higher. Finally, on the crest, his weight was gone too and, with a lightness that was absolute, he shrank to nothingness, disappearing before his own eyes as only someone whose dearest wish has been granted can disappear.

Rettenberger smiles as he passes Kirchstetten. He no longer feels the up and down of the autobahn as simply an interplay between freewheeling and being pulled back, when his small car always seems to get much too slow again; now he takes pleasure in the alternation of fast and slow. He does not increase his lead as he goes up these hills, but his pride grows with the ever-lengthening queue of his pursuers. The helicopter is flying slightly behind him, calmly looking down on the scene.

Tuesday, 22 March 1988. At regular intervals a queue of cars built up at the level crossing. Now and then someone sounded their horn, as if that would hurry the trains up. While the drivers waiting at the lights were impatient to get into the city, you could see that the people coming out of the station had all the time in the world, selecting a particular bouquet or pot-plant outside the flower shops by Simmering Cemetery, or waiting at the tram stop for the 71 or the 72, going in the direction of the main gate of the Central Cemetery.

On the day of his penultimate bank robbery Rettenberger was in one of the few cars at the crossing heading out of the city. He waited, not impatient, but with a certain tingling in his fingers, and looked across at the small Simmering Cemetery, wondering whether the people he could see felt it was a luxury to be able to visit the graves of their loved ones here and not out at the huge Central Cemetery. The village graveyards of his childhood had always seemed creepy places to him.

The bank was on the other side of the level crossing, as if put there specially for him. He could observe the customers going in and out, at the same time imagining another bank robber coming in the opposite direction and holding up the bank before he could get there. What he would do then would be to stay on his tail after he came out, in order to follow his escape and return to private life.

Uphill, downhill. All he can see at any one time is the stretch to the top of the next rise. He has switched the car radio on and has been listening for a while to the local station the farmer had adjusted it to when a song, with a tune and rhymes that would set even the usually mute world of the Alpine foothills singing along, catches his ear: 'You see less at night / when there's no light. / When the sky is blue / ...' Rettenberger sends his laugh out into the broad trough of the valley before him; crazy, the sameness of this landscape! Still, he can handle it when 'you've a much better view.'

After Petersdorf the autobahn makes a long curve to the south, giving a view of the mountains, only to turn back west immediately and continue on another straight past St Pölten. He passes the turn-off to the dual carriageway to Krems, flying into the curve, with all the police cars and vans behind him copying his every move. Each manoeuvre he makes goes back down the line of his pursuers, in a kind of motorised Chinese whispers, until the last vehicle has performed it in its own fashion.

In his small white car, Rettenberger appears at the start of the long St Pölten straight like a proud soldier on horseback, a field marshal. Above him the helicopter, a second one behind that and then the line of blue lights which, despite their impatient flashing, are strangely ineffective, dissipating in the bank of thin cloud.

When he sees the roadblock ahead, his whole body seems to breathe a sigh of relief. The straight is laid out so clearly before him, it gives him a feeling of liberation, even the hill beyond does not lead back into the same landscape but to the levels round Ober-Grafendorf, which stretch as far as St Leonhard. Whilst the rolling hills were so boundless he felt imprisoned by them, it is almost with delight that he heads for the roadblock. He can see the police cars already and a few small figures taking cover. He is driving straight at the crouching policemen. He looks them in the eye; all he can see there is pure fear.

The hunt for the most-wanted criminal in Austria ended on Tuesday, shortly after 3.30 pm. Joseph Rettenberger was on the West Autobahn, heading towards Melk in a Golf he had stolen from a farm near St Christophen. Following him were some fifty police vehicles, above him a helicopter of the federal security services. Police from St Pölten had set up a temporary roadblock by the exit to Mariazell, but Rettenberger had no intention of giving up. He shot through the barrier.

The thin cloud draws a grey veil over the countryside, creating the feeling of floating on air, the only thing that makes the dark weeks of late autumn bearable. There are no more cars between Rettenberger and the roadblock. The field is cleared, but his opponent does not move, while he is racing towards it like a bullet. He already has two-thirds of the straight behind him and the barrier is still there, it does not even appear to get bigger. It will all burst apart if he keeps going straight at those little wire-mesh panels. They will be torn to pieces in the air, as if they were made of paper. His momentum alone will take the weight of the barrier, he does not even need a heavy vehicle, no more than he needs dogged determination or one almighty stamp on the accelerator at the last moment.

The police are nowhere to be seen. He almost thinks he can feel his pursuers' hesitation, while he keeps his car as steady as the helicopter above him, flying towards the roadblock. The only sensation as he drives through it is a brief thump; perhaps he also hears a whistling as the pieces go sailing through the air. Then there's a clattering noise behind him, the pursuing cars have to brake to avoid the falling bits of the barrier, the braking is almost never-ending until the line has come to a halt and the autobahn is quiet once more.

According to reports received so far, shortly after 3.30 Rettenberger broke through a roadblock set up by the St Pölten police on the West Autobahn. Inspector Andreas H., 34, fired at the Golf, as it careered on its way, from a distance of about 50 yards. The bullet penetrated the vehicle in the region of the rear number plate, was deflected and passed through the driver's body before embedding itself in the dashboard. The autopsy revealed that the shot from the officer's Glock pistol had ripped through the driver's heart and lung. Despite that, he still managed to drive another 400 metres.

He has broken through the road block. Not for one moment does his speed seem to have lessened. The road ahead begins to rise gradually. In the oppressive silence all around he can no longer hear the music on the car radio. But the singing is inside his head now. Calm voices, sounding both cautious and determined at the imminent smash. His face is humming along too, his cheeks, his forehead.

Wednesday, 23 March 1988. Everyone is hunting for the man in the mask. Four million in three days! His bag over his shoulder, Rettenberger ran out of the Dornbach branch of the Creditanstalt and up the first side-street. He continued through Schwarzenberg Park and then, on a sudden, crazy inspiration, left his car in the car park and tore up to the top of the ridge forming the edge of the Vienna Woods. He kept to the path along the ridge until he came to the Höhenstrasse, which he ran down, keeping to the left-hand side, while occasional cars whizzed past, tyres thrumming on the cobblestones of the road all Viennese regard as their personal race-track. He reached the Cobenzl. As he looked down on Vienna, as calm as a toy town under a film of haze, in his mind's eye he could see himself continuing along the ridge to the Kahlenberg and the Josefsberg then being swallowed up by the city again after the first traffic lights and crossroads.

It is a relief when, after a few seconds driving on, apparently unaffected, he registers the bullet entering his body, the brief sting of pain as it passes through him. Rettenberger drives on, he wants to make it to the top of the hill leading away from St Pölten, to look down on the flat land below. The car shoots up the rise of its own accord, nothing is required of him, he feels weightless.

A numb silence fills his body. His breast no longer rises as, in obedience to the driving force which has sent him through life in constant haste, he tries to continue breathing. And instead of that minor panic that immediately grips you when you wake up at night gasping for air when there has been too long a gap between breaths, he feels nothing but calm. He is clutching the steering wheel tight. Some of his pursuers are already tearing along after him. The late-autumn mist of the surrounding countryside spreads through his body. Perhaps this hole in his chest could give him a new lease of life. Without fear. What hold-ups there would be! he thinks, smiling to himself. No more nervous breaths before putting on the mask, no more forcing himself, dry-throated, to make his demand for money in as calm and comprehensible voice as possible. He will appear in the bank without a word. The Robber is there and already one person is getting the money out of the safe, while all the others squeeze into a corner. The day's takings are added, like a tip, and he is away, his bulging bag over his shoulder, strolling down the next street, like that bank robber in the Burgenland he read about in the paper on the day of his first robbery.

He cannot keep going like this for long. His body feels tight. He needs air, a lot of air. He is so feeble, so slumped down, he can only just manage to keep his head far enough above the steering wheel to see the immediate stretch of road flying towards him. He reaches the top of the rise, there is the flat land at last, nothing but longing enfolds him. He has arrived.

Only then did he bring the stolen car to an abrupt halt on the hard shoulder. Immediately he was surrounded by the cars of his pursuers. The police officers leapt out and took cover. At that moment a shot rang out. Rettenberger had shot himself in the head, above his right temple. Death was instantaneous.